TESTIMONIALS

"*In The Mosaic, Daniel Levin captures the essence of the human condition in a delightful parable that will entertain, enlighten, and touch the hearts of all who read it. This simple and enjoyable story is a new adventure for all of us who desire to connect with and trust more of what is the same within us all.*"
— *Rev. Dr. Iyanla Van Zant*
New York Times best-selling author; Host of Iyanla Fix My Life (OWN)

"*It is rare that a story today qualifies for the true meaning of a fable but this one does. Like Aesop's Fables, The Mosaic contains one wisdom lesson after another told by characters—some of whom dwell in this world and others in the next. A fun read.*"
— *Caroline Myss*
New York Times best-selling author

"*The Mosaic is a stunning, powerful, timely and magnificent book. The Juiceman . . . Road Worker . . . the Traveler . . . the Street Artist . . . the characters, archetypes, and metaphors within this brilliant fable are intoxicating, mesmerizing, and heart expanding. Daniel Levin provides deeper messages through the 'back door' of our own consciousness, resulting in subtle and precious heart-warming take-aways. Highly recommended.*"
— *Arielle Ford with Brian Hillard* Best-selling author
Relationship Expert and Leading Personality in the Self-Growth Movement

The most profound and lasting way to learn is through story, and a story that reflects so many aspects of our shared human journey keeps the lessons learned alive in the heart forever. This is one such beautiful and lasting story."

— Sonia Choquette
New York Times best-selling author

"When author Daniel Levin told me that The Mosaic was a parable about one boy's search for heaven, the people he meets along the way and the lessons he learns, I was skeptical that anyone could make this archetypal hero's journey fresh, new and engaging. The Mosaic blew away my skepticism in the first few pages. Every person our hero "Mo" encounters from the Trashman to the Wise One spoke directly to my soul. I loved meeting the Blind Woman and the Shoemaker, the Ordinaries and the Specials, and had one deep insight after another as Levin deftly wove each character's profound knowledge into the fabric of the parable, never once sounding preachy or resorting to platitudes. I've been a student and a teacher of self-awareness and transformation for over 40 years, and reading The Mosaic was truly a highlight of my own personal journey. The magic it imparts is palpable and the possibilities it ignites are real."

— Debra Poneman
Best-selling author; Founder of Yes to Success Seminars; Co-founder of Your Year of Miracles

"The Mosaic is a beautiful story with a profound message: Look past all the seemingly segmented parts of our lives and ourselves and find the unity and connectedness within the bigger picture."

— Bruce D. Schneider
Founder, Ipec Coaching and Best-selling Author

"The Mosaic is a remarkable parable for our time. Daniel Levin's luscious writing style echoes of the Alchemist, as it radiates with joy and guides you on an adventure of the heart. The deeper messages in this book come as a gentle breeze and invite you into the garden of your soul. The Mosaic has lasting magic for the ages!"
— **Denise Linn**
Best-selling author of Sacred Space

"The Mosaic is a delightful read and a powerful metaphor that speaks to the human condition. Mo's journey, his search for heaven and the lessons he learned along the way, mirror our own personal journey to self-awakening. Thanks Daniel Levin for weaving such a masterpiece about our interconnectedness, the possibilities it creates and the opportunity it presents for us to share and learn from our doubts, fears, pains, joys and successes."
— **Devon Harris**
Three-time and Original Jamaican bobsled Olympian; Speaker, Author

"The Mosaic. I knew it would be different. I knew it would open doors of insight and pathways to truth, because Danny IS different, and that's what Danny does. What I did not expect is the extent to which the Mosaic draws you in with every step on that winding journey, how it connects to our own personal experiences, every raw, searing, emotional loss, with each of our own personal joys, our insecurities, our triumphs! Mo is in all of us. Mo's journey, his pathway, metaphorically, is the journey we all have walked or will walk someday, in some way—if we allow ourselves the freedom to see and experience even that which 'we cannot see.' The Mosaic, in every chapter, touches a chord in our souls, it connects us and it is a beautiful experience."
— **Hillary Alexander**
Permanent Secretary for MSET - Jamaican Government

"The Mosaic offers you an opportunity to go on an adventure. I had to read it slowly to absorb it all and it moved me to tears in moments. It offers deeper insights into our own personal and planetary transformation. There is ageless wisdom in Levin's stories, and he weaves them together effortlessly. I read the chapters to my children and discussed the ideas throughout and it opened a wonderland of conversations. There are those books that come at the right time and this is one of them. The Mosaic is a gorgeous book, one that you feel yourself into and then absorb the gems."
— *Rhea Lalla*
CEO & Founder at Build Great Minds

"You had me at The Mortician! From the opening chapter of The Mosaic, I was captivated. Anyone who has ever experienced loss will no doubt relate to the emotions of Mo from the early pages of The Mosaic til the very end. Mo's journey of self discovery is, in some ways, a journey we all take to varying degrees throughout our lives. Levin weaves an enticing tale as we follow Mo's journey and the colourful characters he learns from along the way. An absorbing read."
— *Trent Munday, SVP*
International Mandara Spa & Steiner Spa Consulting

"The Mosaic will immerse you in a universe where everyone and everything is connected. Every page you turn will delight you."
— *Elena Baranova*
Partner, Right Magic Films, Inc.

"The Mosaic takes you on an incredible journey of self-awakening. I found myself walking together with the main character, allowing the unfolding process of life to take place in me just as it was with Mo. I realized over and over again that we are all truly connected. Danny's wisdom is in his ability to take the reader on a meaningful life journey through the interaction with his characters. It is his gift."
— **Elena Bensonoff**
Pharmacist, Artisan Perfumer, Spiritual Health Practitioner

"Daniel Levin's words and story-weaving resemble the majesty and simplicity of Coelho with the capacity to touch the human heart just as deeply."
— **Kylie Slavik**
Copywriter and Storyteller

"The Mosaic is like taking a walk with your soul. It is a journey not to be missed."
— **Jody Doty**
Soul Reader

"Like the Alchemist, this is a book that speaks to the heart. The elegant simplicity of the storytelling woven beautifully with universal lessons makes this book hard to put down. I felt moved, inspired, and connected to the stories and characters of The Mosaic. Thank you for reminding us each person and experience in our lives is magically leading us to exactly where we need to be. I hope this beautiful work reaches the hands of millions."
— **Neelam Verma**
Television Host, Speaker, Entrepreneur

As we travel with Mo through all of his life's building-blocks, it is impossible not to see yourself---your own growth, pain, love and joy. What I truly relish about The Mosaic is the follow through of feelings. It hits such depth. Daniel Levin's writing resonates to remind us that not only are we on our journey but so are our great teachers. The Mosaic fixes itself to be one of the great dog-eared, much-loved books of our time."
— **Heather Carlucci**
Chef, Medium, Medical Intuitive

"There are a lot of self-help books out there but only a few qualify as life-changers. Within the first couple of pages, I was already in tears. It is extremely relatable. You will find yourself saying, 'That's me!' The Mosaic isn't one of those books you read once, think it's great and put it on the shelf. The characters and the lessons stay with you. This is what makes it a life-changing book. I have two others like this that I give to friends when I think they need something; this book will be the third. The Mosaic will help more people than you could have ever dreamed."
— **Natalie Elis Diasti**
Screenwriter

"The Mosaic is more than a book to be read; it is full of lessons to live. It offers us the opportunity to see life as an adventure that, when approached with an open mind and heart, can lead us to a far richer experience than we might have imagined for ourselves."
— **Maria Dell'Isola**
Public Relations Consultant, Freelance Writer and Editor

"I love this book. It talks to me. I have connected with many of its characters and they have inspired me greatly. The Mosaic is a book I will keep by my bed and read over and over."
— *Shervin Hojat*
Engineer

"Many times I found myself reading through tears as the book resonated on such a deep level. Don't be fooled by its simplicity, the message is well thought out and sophisticated."
— *Biba John*
Instructor – Grand Canyon University

THE
MOSAIC

Also by *Daniel Bruce Levin*

The Mosaic Archetype Card Deck
Receive Messages from the Archetypes of Your Personal Mosaic

El Mosaico
Spanish Edition E-book
Translated by Ana Laura Levin

The Mosaic Audio
Read by the author

The Mosaic Newsletter
Innovation I FutureThinking I Connection

The Mosaic Online Course
The strategy and delivery of creating your
personal and business Mosaic

The Mosaic Retreat
Total Immersion into the creation of your
personal and business Mosaic

The Mosaic Workshop
A 1/2 day, full day or 3 day event that integrates
all the pieces of you or your businesses Mosaic

For more information, please visit:
www.DanielBruceLevin.com
www.TheMosaicOnline.com

or email: zenseidanny@me.com

An Extraordinary Tale of the Absolutely Ordinary

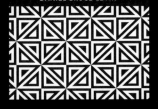

Daniel Bruce Levin

Published by Waterside Press
Encinitas, CA 92024

Printed in Canada

CONTENTS

ACKNOWLEDGEMENTS

For Mom and Dad
who I see now, never left me.

For Ana Laura Levin—My ALL.
You found me at the bottom of my life and lifted me up.
You are my heart and my soul. Your love makes me feel invincible.

Elisa Levin
You are my greatest gift and my teacher. You are unconditional love.
I may never really know what you think or how you feel,
but I know you and in knowing you, I am complete.

Valentino and Camila
Thank you for showing me my love could be bigger than what I knew.

Sandra Sedgbeer—My Muse.
You believed in me and reminded me that I am a storyteller.
You told me to tell my story and it became this fable.

Bill Gladstone—My Agent and My Publisher.
You always believed in The Mosaic, you took me under your wing
and brought this work of my heart to the world. Thank You.

Alexia Paul
For balancing reality and mystical, and cutting away all
that did not belong.

And most of all, this book is dedicated to *You, The Reader*.
For it is your stories that inspire me most,
you are a constant reminder to me that we are all more than we appear.
You are the heartbeat of The Mosaic.
You are the meaning that makes this story come alive.
Your stories will touch millions, and in them, we see
we are all connected.

This is The Mosaic.

To the real Mo
who lives within all of us.

PREFACE

If I can be vulnerable with you,
and completely honest, I didn't write this book at all.

Somewhere along the line,
The Mosaic came alive within me,
guiding my hands to type the words *it* wanted me to say.

Many of the characters were familiar to me—
I had met them over the course of my life—
but others I was meeting only for the first time,
much like you, the reader, are meeting them now.

If The Mosaic does its job well,
the story it tells will not only be mine, but yours as well.
It is my hope that you will get to know its characters,
and that you will call on them
when and if you need them.

The fact that you are holding this book in your hands right now
means it has already found you.
You are a piece of The Mosaic's artistry.
It has come for you.

You are not alone.
Invite *your* characters into your life.
Listen to their stories
for they will show you things you have never seen before.
See what cannot be seen.
This is the secret of The Mosaic

Welcome.

THE MORTICIAN

Mo would never forget the first time he saw The Mortician.
He appeared in Mo's dream
at exactly the same moment that
Mo's father took his last breath, many miles away.

Seeing the dark man standing next to his father
sent a chill through Mo's body,
and left no doubt in his mind that his father's life was over.

That's why what happened next shocked him.

Awakened from the dream, The Mortician was gone.
Standing in front of him with outstretched arms,
just as he had so many times before,
was his dad.
But as much as everything seemed the same,
it was all different.
His father's eyes filled with the tears that come
when you know
you will never see who you are looking at again.

Mo wanted it to be like it used to be.
He wanted to run and jump into his father's arms
and give him the biggest, fullest body hug a boy could ever give.
He wanted to laugh with him until late into the night,
but the look in his father's eyes,
the expression on his face, told Mo
that this was not a time for laughter.

With his eyebrows tucked in, and his gaze one inch above Mo's head,
he spoke words Mo had never heard him speak before.

Everything about his voice was different—
the volume, the cadence, and the intensity.

It was as if these words were meant to prepare Mo
for something that was still to come.
Each was spoken with a precision
that carved its way into Mo's memory.

"My time here is over, Mo.
You are ready.
I have done what I was brought here to do.
What you need now, I cannot give you.
Soon, others will come to guide you.
Do not be distracted by how they look or what they do.
Nothing is as it seems.
I have prepared you, for you are not like the others.
You see things they do not see and hear what they do not hear.

"Be vigilant with all, even the voices that live in your own head.
Always listen, but do not always follow.
When you meet those who can guide you,
follow them.

"There will be times when you feel you can't trust yourself.
Trust yourself anyway.
There will be times when you feel completely alone.
Know this: you are not alone.
In time, more will be given to you, and you will understand.

"Mo, I must go now, but I will never leave you.
Though my time here is over,

I will always be with you.
Things are not what they seem."

As these final words left his mouth, Mo's father was gone.

On the long ride home from summer camp,
Mo prayed and prayed that his dream wasn't true,
but the voice within him
and the tears that flowed down his cheeks told him otherwise.

He asked his aunt and uncle
who had come to take him home,
"What happened?
Why have you come?"
But no matter how many times he asked on the 10-hour drive south,
he received the same answer:
"Your mom asked us to come and get you.
That is all we know."

When finally he opened the door to his house,
he hoped to see his father sitting
in the burnt orange chair where he sat every night
with a drink in his hand, listening to the radio.
But the chair was empty.

Mo ran through the people who crowded the cramped, hot rooms.
"What are they doing here?" he thought,
looking for what he already knew he would not find.

When he found his mother in the kitchen,
he ran towards her and asked,
"Mom, Mom, where's Dad?"

And when he saw the tears in her eyes,
he said, "Mom, are you ok?"
As she hugged him tight, she burst into tears
and said, "Your father is gone."

In the past, no matter how bad things were,
she always knew how to say things
in just the right way to comfort him.
But today her words did not bring comfort.

The torrential flood of tears
she expected to pour from Mo's eyes
did not come,
and it troubled her.

Moments later, it was he who spoke words of comfort to her.
And for just a moment, through her tears, she smiled inside, thinking,
"He is his mother's son."

His tears finally came
in the late hours of the night, when one day turns into the next.
The table next to his bed held a framed picture of his dad.
The glass was cracked and the picture now torn.
The uncontrollable pain inside him could be quieted no longer.
There, in the solitude of his bed,
covered with blankets,
he screamed silent screams from the core of his gut,
screams that no one but the silence could hear.

The finality of it all struck him.
He would never sit again
waiting for the turn of his father's hand on the doorknob,

never run and jump into his outstretched arms to welcome him home.
He would never again walk with him,
and laugh with him late into the night.
He was gone.

And just as he was falling asleep,
he saw his father just long enough
to remind Mo of the words he had spoken previously.
"Do not be sad, Mo.
I have done what I was brought here to do.
What you need now, I cannot give you.
Soon, others will come to guide you."

Mo wondered who these others were
and how they would come.
When the gift of sleep finally arrived,
it took him while he was praying
that those who would guide him would come soon.

THE ROAD WORKER

Mo awoke before the sun, torn.
He was still the naïve,
innocent 13-year-old boy he had been the day before,
but he was no longer a child
whose parents protected him from the troubled world around him.

His dad had died and now everything was different.

He sat and waited for his mom to wake up,
but when he heard the sound
of his friends playing in the schoolyard down the street,
he knew it was time to get going.

But Mo did not go to play in the schoolyard.
That was a place for kids.
Instead, he went out looking for a way to make money
so he and his mother could survive.
Mo had always known,
the way children sometimes sense these things,
that his dad had been unwise in the ways of money.
He had died, the owner of one black suit,
and a world of debt.

Even so, Mo's dad was his hero and he felt a responsibility
to fix the situation for the sake of his father's legacy.

So, as his friends ran and laughed with childhood innocence,
Mo went searching for work.
For some reason, he chose to walk away
from the crowded city,
on an isolated, two-lane road leading off into the country.

Houses were soon replaced with vast fields of crops guarded by forests.
"Strange," he thought. "Why did I go this way when all the jobs are in town?"
For much of the walk, he chastised himself for going the wrong way.

The quiet of the winding country road did not last long.
Around each turn lurked the demon of his fears and insecurities.
The voice grew louder as it yelled at him,
"What are you doing? You will never get a job like this!
You are a kid who doesn't know anything about work.
Your parents did everything for you. What do you know how to do?"

The faster he ran, the louder the voice grew.
He wondered how it kept up with him,
when he realized the voice was coming from inside him.

"I'm going to turn around and go back home," he thought.
And then he heard the voice begin to shriek once again.
"That's right," it said. *"Go home to your Mommy.*
You can't do this.
Even if somehow you talk someone into hiring you, you won't last a day.
You're not good enough.
You don't know how to do anything!"
Mo knew this voice,
the voice of his weakness.
But today he fought it, saying,
"I know there isn't much I can do,
but I have to find something.
I will keep looking until something comes along."

But the demon of doubt would not quiet.
Despair hit him,

and he cried out from the most broken part of his heart,
asking his father,
"How could you leave me?"

The pain he felt as those words left his lips
brought a tremble that shook his entire body.
His father had told him
there would be times like this
when he would feel alone.
What he did not tell him
was how scared it would make him feel,
or how empty.

Then, in the distance,
he heard the rhythmic pounding punches
of what sounded like a jackhammer.
Walking toward the sound,
he saw a man working in the middle of the road.

As Mo approached, The Road Worker asked,
"Are you ok?"
Mo for some reason answered,
"Yes. Yes," though it clearly wasn't true.
He wanted to tell this man everything—how his dad had died,
and how he left home early this morning to find a job
to help pay the family expenses.
He wanted to ask The Road Worker if he would hire him,
to tell him if he did he would not be sorry.
But what he said next was, "The truth is I am not really ok."

The Road Worker turned off his jackhammer.
He needed a little break anyway;
he had been working all morning and his body was tired.
And the boy clearly needed a friendly face, and a story to feel better.
He began:

"I am a Road Worker.
Like my father and his father before him,
I work days that are long and grueling, but never have I complained.
I feel thankful to have a job that allows me to take care of my family."

As Mo listened to his story, he thought,
"Maybe I did go the right way.
Walking away from town seemed crazy,
but now listening to The Road Worker, I feel hope.
He is doing exactly what I need to do.
Who knows, maybe he is the one who will help me."

The Road Worker, leaning on his jackhammer, continued,
"It is hard.
Many days, I leave before my children awake
and arrive home after they have already gone to bed.
But every night, I go into their room,
kiss them on the forehead,
and whisper to them how much I love them.

"My wife tells me
every morning when they awake, they race to the mirror
and look for the tiny smudges of grease and grime
my unwashed lips have left on their faces.
They then come to the table, laughing,
knowing that their father

had come to them without their knowing
in the middle of the night and left his mark.
Every time my wife tells me this story, I feel happy."

Mo felt his father's love in these words,
and the more The Road Worker spoke, the more Mo missed him.
A tear gathered in Mo's eye as The Road Worker continued.
"Sometimes, when I finish work early
and the others go to drink a beer,
I race home,
hoping to see the kids before they go to sleep.

"When I arrive and they are still awake,
I rouse them from their beds
and we talk and laugh
late into the night,
staying up way longer than we should."

Mo remembered doing exactly the same thing with his father,
and he wondered if all dads did this,
or if The Road Worker and his dad
were just connected in some way.

"On those nights," The Road Worker continued,
"as I place them back in bed,
they look me in the eye and say:
'Dad, when we grow up, we want to be road workers just like you.'"

"I have heard of families
where the parents work hard
to give their children
a chance to have a better life.

But, honestly, I cannot think of a better life
than the life our family already has."

Mo thought to himself, "*If I had not grown up in my house
I would have chosen to live with The Road Worker.*"

Mo knew it was not nice to interrupt,
but the little voice within him could no longer be contained.
He wanted The Road Worker to know his story.
He shared with him the death of his father,
and his mother's devastation at the loss.

Quiet settled in and when his tears subsided,
he asked The Road Worker
if he might know of any work he could do.
Mo admitted that he was young and inexperienced,
but he was willing to work hard and do whatever he was told to do.

The Road Worker paused.
He noticed the silky smooth hands of the boy,
but he liked him.
While kids his age were out playing games,
Mo was trying to find a job to help his family survive.
This, more than his soft hands, showed his character.
The Road Worker was as proud of him
as he would have been of one of his own sons.
He observed Mo for a long time,
then said with confidence:

"I admire you, Mo,
and I would be honored if you would work with me.

But you have to know, this is hard work.
Your body will ache,
especially in the beginning.
There will be nights when you will think you do not have the strength
to come back the next day.
But you must come back.
Every morning before the sun rises,
I will count on you being here.

"If you accept my offer, you must find the strength within you
that will push you to show up
when your mind and body say you can't.
There are days it will be hard, Mo.
But if you are like me, it will be rewarding.
It will help you become a man.

"I expect only that you show up and work hard.
In return, I will pay your family's bills.
You will never have to worry about that again."

Mo eagerly accepted The Road Worker's offer
and listened as The Road Worker continued

"Every road in life, no matter how beautiful, has its potholes.
And though each pothole presents a different set of challenges,
the solution is almost always the same:
Chip off the bumps, fill in the ruts,
and get to the other side.

"What strikes me most is not the potholes themselves,
but how people respond to them.

"Over the years, I have watched many people.
Some see the pothole and drive around it.
Others drive right into it,
assess the damage,
and do whatever it takes to get their car fixed.
Still others drive into it,
damage the front end of their car,
and never admit that something needs to be fixed.
They drive, hoping no one will notice.
But everyone notices.

"The ones who interest me the most
are those who drive into the pothole
and never leave.
They get stuck there.
They forget how alluring the road has been
with all its twists and turns and ups and downs,
and they cannot see that
the road on the other side of this pothole is awe-inspiring,
filled with possibilities and opportunities.

"They get stuck.
And they start to believe
that there is no way out,
that the road will never be smooth again…

"I am a Road Worker
and I assure you,
no matter how bad it seems,
every pothole
one day will again become a smooth road."

With that, Mo ran to The Road Worker,
hesitated a moment, as if to see if it was alright,
thanked him and then gave him a big hug.

Mo had left his house that morning in search of a solution
with no idea what, if anything, he would find.
As he stood now with The Road Worker,
not only had he found an answer
better than he could have ever imagined,
but he felt the presence of his dad in the The Road Worker.

When Mo returned home,
he wanted to tell his mother how scared he had been on his walk,
of the voices he'd heard and the victory he'd had.
He wanted to share with her The Road Worker,
and tell her everything that had happened.
But it was already late,
and his mom was once again asleep.
He went to her room, walked up to her bed,
quietly gave her a kiss, and told her how much he loved her.

When she awoke, the sun was up and Mo was already gone.
All she noticed was a tiny smudge of grease and grime on her cheek.

Somewhere, unseen, Mo's father smiled.

Every day Mo came home from working on the road
feeling pain in parts of his body that he never even knew existed.
Every morning he woke up, and his body said,
"I cannot endure any more pain."
Caught in the battle of cross purposes that raged within him,

he chose doing good for others over what he wanted.
As noble as his choice seemed,
it laid the groundwork for problems that would later plague him.

But there was another ache.
It went deeper than the discomfort of his body,
and began to torment his soul.
He couldn't put his finger on it,
but all the same he knew something wasn't right.
The hours he put in every day to make sure the bills got paid
solved one problem but created another.

He should have noticed it sooner,
but because most evenings
he arrived home late, after his mom had already gone to bed,
and most mornings he left before she woke up,
he didn't see it coming.
Tired and sore, most nights he would skip dinner
and climb straight into bed.
More often than not,
he was asleep before his head hit the pillow.

But it was on the other nights,
the ones when he arrived home early enough
to sit and eat dinner with his mother,
that he noticed something was wrong.
She spent most of her time alone,
and she was becoming more and more disconnected.
It happened so gradually,
the deviation was imperceptible at first.
But the more Mo watched her, the more he saw something was amiss.

One evening, as the second Christmas without his dad approached,
Mo and his mother sat at the dinner table.
Though he feared the answer,
he asked, "How are you, mom?"

She sighed, then said, "I am sorry, Mo,
at how distant I have become.
I miss him so much."
She paused for a long moment and then continued,
"And then on top of that,
I am completely overwhelmed
by the enormity of the debt we are in.

Whereas, normally I am strong,
I see no solution.
I want to be here for you,
but I am tired and feel like giving up."

Hearing this was devastating.
Tears filled Mo's eyes and rolled down his cheeks.
When he hugged her,
their tears merged and cascaded down her cheeks.
He sat for what seemed like forever holding her.

When he was sure the tears had passed,
he whispered in her ear,
"Mom, our debt is nearly behind us.
Between my work and The Road Worker's kind help,
we are almost in the clear."

Mo pulled his head back to look at her.
He was sure he would see relief,

but his mother just smiled a lifeless smile
and without any emotion said,
"That's great, Mo. That's really great."
He realized he had missed the point
as she retreated to the burnt orange chair in the living room
and lost herself
in the big box of photographs she kept there.

Each picture told a story,
and the memory it created
fell like a domino into another memory,
and all of the stories tumbled into the one story
of the man she had loved and missed beyond measure.

The pictures made her feel closer to him,
and she sat all day looking at them,
telling him how much she missed him,
and how soon she would again be in his arms.
Somehow she knew he could hear her.

The photo she was looking at now
had been taken less than a month before he died.
It was a picture of them all laughing
around the dining room table together, late one night.

The next day, Mo arrived at work early.
He had spent the night restlessly tossing and turning,
punishing himself for thinking he had figured it all out,
when in fact, he had gotten it all wrong.

He'd felt a grace descend,
and lift him up when there was no way out.

But the hours he spent away working
only intensified his mother's feelings of being alone,
and her aloneness grew hour by hour.

When The Road Worker arrived
at the small shed where they kept their tools it was still dark,
but as he approached, he could feel the heaviness in the air.
Something was different.
It wasn't that Mo was already there;
it was more than that.
As The Road Worker came closer, he could feel
Mo's agitation and uneasiness.
Something was definitely wrong.

It reminded him of the first time they'd met.
Instinctively, The Road Worker came over
to the bench in the back of the dim shed
and put his arm around Mo's shoulder.

Suddenly he was no longer The Road Worker,
but a father trying to protect his son from a terrible pain.
He pulled Mo closer to his chest and held him.
That embrace, which he would never again feel from his father,
brought a new wave of tears to Mo's eyes,
and exposed a hole in Mo's heart that could never be repaired.

The Road Worker knew these tears
had been held inside Mo for a very long time.
As he held Mo, he told him, "Let the tears come.
Cry on my shoulder until no more tears will come."
The Road Worker continued, "I will always be here for you, Mo."

Mo had no idea how to tell The Road Worker he was leaving.
So he just decided to tell the truth,
and between the exhalation and the inhalation of his next breath,
he looked at The Road Worker and shared with him the words of his heart.
"I do not know where I would have been without you.
When everything in my world fell apart, you were there.
You taught me much more than the way of The Road Worker,
and though I am sure there is a lot for me to still learn,
I must go.

"My mother is not well. I thought I was helping,
but I have made everything worse.
I have no idea how we will survive,
but being constantly away from her
has caused her to feel even more disconnected from life.
She sits all day looking at pictures of a life that used to be,
and has no relationship to the life that is.
I must spend my days with her,
because honestly, I do not know how many more she has left."

The Road Worker put away the tools and walked Mo into the city.
Both of them prayed silently for the other as they walked,
and neither said a word.

On most days, at the entrance to the city stood a mobile juice bar,
and The Road Worker hoped today
The Juiceman would be there,
and that he would be able to give Mo something.

THE JUICEMAN

As they approached the teeming city,
The Road Worker smiled.
In the distance, he saw The Juiceman
pedaling his mobile juice bar across the train tracks.
The Road Worker's prayers were now of gratitude.
He knew The Juiceman would know the right thing to say.

The lines etched in the face
of the man before him
brought Mo out of his prayers and contemplation,
and into the experiences buried within The Juiceman's face,
each wrinkle a testament
to a life of challenge, courage, and determination.
Each he was sure had a story he wanted to hear.

Though the man's body held the strength of one much younger,
the looseness of the threads on his clean, pressed clothes
gave away more than their age.

Mo knew
life for this man had not been
as easy as the smile on his face
or the gleam in his eye would lead others to believe.

The fact that he peddled
from the other side
of the imaginary line
that separated the prosperous
from those who would never make it out of poverty
did not seem to matter to the people of the town.

A line formed in front of his juice cart
the moment he arrived
at his usual corner under the thick oak trees.
And as he served his customers gladly,
he listened to their frustrations
and the stories of their lives.
Every once in a while,
he would smile and make a comment.

Mo stood with The Road Worker
at the end of the line and watched, entranced.
The words of his father in his dream came to him again,
'You see what others do not see and hear things they do not hear.
Listen to what you hear, and see what you see.'
There was something remarkable about The Juiceman.

He bided his time, and when his turn came,
and The Road Worker introduced Mo,
Mo looked deep into The Juiceman's eyes, and softly remarked,

"I have been watching you for some time
and in every case,
I saw that no matter how a person came to you,
they left happier.
Who are you, Juiceman?
And what magic do you weave for them
while they are here with you?"

The Juiceman's face started to crease
and then a big belly laugh erupted from his insides.
When his laugh quieted,

he looked to his friend The Road Worker and said,
"I have no idea what your little friend here is talking about.
I am a Juiceman from the other side of town.
My job is simple.
I squeeze things until what is inside them comes out."

Mo looked over to smile at The Road Worker.
He wanted to tell him he understood what The Juiceman was saying,
but The Road Worker had already started his journey back to the road.
The sun had been up for a while by now,
and there was still much work to do.
Mo wanted to run after The Road Worker—
there was so much more he wanted to tell him—
but just then the corners of The Juiceman's mouth twitched slightly,
and he cocked his head and said,
"The oranges I use to make my juice take years to grow.
First a seed is planted in a small container
and given sunlight and water.
The seed is carefully monitored until it starts to grow.
Then it is moved into a bigger container
so that it can become a little tree.

"Over time, when the little tree becomes strong enough,
it is transplanted from the container into the earth.
There it grows big and bears fruit for all to enjoy.
Each step in this long process is necessary
to produce a fruit of good quality.
And yet, it's only when the fruit is taken from the tree
that it can truly be enjoyed.

"I am a Juiceman.
I do not know how to do much,

but I have learned how to squeeze an orange,
and in doing that,
I have also learned how to live a life.
For, you see, the way we do anything is the way we do everything."

He held up the rind of a squeezed orange to illustrate his point.
"This is how most live their lives.
They squeeze the orange from the middle
but leave a lot of fruit around the edges.
They live safely, never going after all that life offers,
never venturing out of what they know.

"But, Mo, I have been blessed
to be able to cross the tracks and be accepted.
I have been allowed to mix with the affluent,
and I have learned from them.
The way they live life
has taught me to go all the way to the edge
to squeeze out of the orange everything it has to give.

"They see every moment as an opportunity,
and understand when they do not use all they are given,
they will not be given any more.

"Mo, everything in life changes.
One moment the orange is on the tree, the next moment it gets picked,
and in another moment, it is eaten or made into a juice.
What is now will no longer be.

"Enjoy what is now,
and know soon it will be gone."

With that, he handed Mo a glass of freshly squeezed orange juice
and said, as Mo reached into his pocket to pay for it,

"The Road Worker has already paid for your juice,
and he also gave me something to give to you three weeks ago."
He told me, 'I will bring to you a boy.
When I leave, he will try to come after me.
Do not let him.
After I am gone,
please give him this envelope.'"

When Mo opened the envelope, he could not believe his eyes.
Just this morning
as he came to talk to The Road Worker
he had thought,
"Without my job, how will we ever escape this life of poverty?"
But now inside the envelope
there was more money than he could have ever imagined.

There was so much more Mo wanted to say to The Juiceman,
but there were others now standing in line
who needed to have their time with him.

For a moment, Mo felt calm,
as if life were giving him a second chance,
but each step he took
brought him face to face with the pain of knowing
he was not a strong enough reason for his mom to stay.

On the long walk home along the city streets,
he found himself lost in thoughts of his dad.
He wondered if it were possible

to create such a strong connection with another person
that time and space could not break it.

He and his mom had felt so connected to his dad,
but when he passed,
both of them felt something within them shatter.
Mo wondered if people in heaven felt whole or shattered,
or if there was a glue up there
that made the broken pieces whole again.
Now that he was gone, Mo realized his dad had been the glue
that held the pieces of the family together.

What troubled Mo even more was that all his life
people told him he was just like his dad.
But in this moment, he found no similarity.
Try as he might, he could provide no glue to hold things together.
Everything Mo had done, every sacrifice he had made,
he did with the intent to make his mother's life better,
but she didn't want life.

Mo's dad had died in her arms while making love to her,
And in that moment her life had died with him.
It meant nothing to her without him.
All she wanted was to reconnect to the love story
she treasured above all else.

As Mo entered onto the dusty street
that led to his home,
he saw through his tear-filled eyes in the distance,
a man standing by the door.
For a moment, he thought his wish was granted,
and that his dad had come to make everything right.

THE MORTICIAN

As he ran toward the door,
it was not his father he saw,
but The Mortician he had seen in his dream.

This time The Mortician was real,
standing in front of him
on the cold cement porch.
His eyes were dark and penetrating,
but his words were kind and full of compassion
as he told Mo what he did not want to hear.

"Prepare yourself, Mo.
Your mother's time here now is short;
be with her as much as you can.
She will develop an illness that cannot be cured.
In six months she will be gone."

Mo could hardly breathe
as The Mortician put a firm hand on his shoulder before turning to go.
In the distance, a car backfired
and a dog barked.
Mo sat down and held his head in his hands.

Six months to that day, she died,
on Independence Day.
She passed on the same day as her love had, two years previously.
Both parents dying on the same day had to be a message,
but Mo found no meaning in it.
He wondered why his mom had not taken the time to
explain it to him before she died,
or come to him later in a vision, like his dad had.

From the depths of his despair, he promised himself
he would find the place called heaven,
where the well-meaning adults told him his parents now lived.
He would let nothing get in his way,
and even though it troubled him
that he had no idea where it was or how to get there,
he knew in order to feel connected again, he had to find it.

THE TRAVELER

Mo had no idea how long he had sat in the overgrown yard
in front of his house
or how long she had been watching him.
Her step made no sound as it touched the ground.
The line of her body never wrinkled,
such was the grace and lightness of her movement.

When he did finally see her
as she emerged out of the darkening shadows,
he could not help but notice the depth of her penetrating brown eyes.
There was power in those eyes,
and Mo could feel it enter him.

They stood together for some time
enjoying the conversation silence can bring.
When she finally spoke, she did so without saying a word.
Somehow, her thoughts were going right into his head.

Mo was taken by this.
He had in the past heard things that others did not hear,
but he had never heard a person's thoughts.
He wanted to see if he could send thoughts to her too,
so he decided to mentally ask her a question.

"Woman who speaks without talking, who are you?
And what is so important for me to hear
that you placed your thoughts in my head?"

Immediately Mo heard, "I am The Traveler."
And for just a moment, as day inched toward night,
the boy in him reveled in the fact

that they were able to communicate this way.
He wondered if he could do this with others, too.

Her voice in his head now carried an authority
that brought him back.
"Pardon me for eavesdropping," she said with a coy smile.
"I heard you say you are committed to finding a place,
but you have no idea where it is or how to find it.

"Over the years, I have found many places others could not find.
If you truly want to find heaven,
I would be happy to help you," The Traveler said.

"Yes. Yes. Yes.
I would love your help," Mo said.
"When can we start?" he asked
with both excitement and a little trepidation.
The Traveler's smile was now not coy but comforting,
and it helped to put his mind at ease.
He forgot that she could read his thoughts
and was a bit embarrassed that she had seen his fear.

"The journey has already begun.
Our first destination is not a place, but a change of thought.
Even now as we speak, the change has begun."

They stood together on the small patch of grass for a few minutes,
neither saying a word,
but something was definitely happening.
It was subtle, but Mo could feel it.
A pain was being lifted from him effortlessly,
and he could feel his heart opening.

When he spoke, the words he said to The Traveler surprised him.
He shared things with her he had never shared with anyone,
things that before now even he had not known.

"When my father died, I died too.
I shut down that day.
Nothing out there interested me anymore.
All I wanted was to go back in time
and be with my dad."

"I completely understand," said The Traveler.
"His connection meant everything to you.
And when you lost that connection, nothing else mattered.
You wanted it back. You still do.
You never got the time you needed to mourn.
Instead, you blamed yourself for something that was not real,
and you created stories
that tore apart your soul,
stories of not being worthy.

"It wasn't that your mom's connection to you
wasn't strong enough to make her stay,
it was that she never let go of her connection to him even when he died.
Time and space had no power over their love.
Even the fact that they lived in parallel realities
couldn't keep them apart."

The more she spoke, the more her words touched him.
He knew of this love, but since the death of his father,
Mo had hidden the desire to feel it behind high walls
as a way to protect himself, so that he would never be hurt by it again.

The Traveler's words found their way into him.
"It's time to walk, Mo.
Gather your belongings, though you will not need much.
We will head south together.
Do you see the reddening edges of the dogwood?
Fall is coming, followed by winter,
and we will go where it is warm."

Mo left her slight figure waiting and went in to gather his things.
He looked around his sparse childhood home,
and felt the tug of the familiar
pull against his desire to go—to find what he was seeking.
He filled a small bag with pieces of the broken picture frame
and the photo of his dad, as well as some provisions.
An hour later, they were on a country road
leaving his home town.

He noticed her watching him as he walked,
and suddenly his stride felt different.
There was an effortlessness to his step
that he had never before noticed,
and this made him happy.

Intriguingly, her pace matched his perfectly.
He wondered if it was something she was doing or just coincidental,
so he lengthened his stride to try to create some distance,
and her stride lengthened, too.
Playfully, trying to catch her off guard, he quickly slowed down,
but again her pace matched his and she remained right beside him.
They walked like this for quite a while, side by side,
in a harmonious dance.

The empty road,
lit only by starlight and a crescent moon,
led them out of the city and down into a valley.
Mo could contain his thought no longer and asked,
"How are you able to mirror my pace so exactly?"

"Over the years," she said with a grin.
"I have walked with many people,
and I studied the way they walk.
I became a student of their steps,
and I have learned much about the way of walking.
As we've walked together, have you noticed anything different?"

"Yes," Mo replied. "My steps are more effortless, more enjoyable."

"Hmmmm," The Traveler replied.
"Watching people walk taught me something very important.
Every step must have a beginning, a middle, and an end.
Without each, there can be no step.

"When people follow this simple pattern, their walk is effortless.
It is only when they try to skip one that life goes out of sync."

"She is guiding my steps. That's why it's so effortless," Mo thought.

The Traveler continued,
the only sound the dirt road crunching under their feet.
"In order for something to begin, another thing must end.
It is the way of nature.
Day replaces night.
What is empty becomes filled, and that which is filled becomes empty.

But there are those who try to hold on to what was.
They do not want to let go of something that has already ended.
They think they can make the day last longer,
but the day does not worry about what they think.
When it is time for it to end, it ends.
And nothing they can do can change this simple reality.
What ends, ends.
But those who want to hold on to the day
do not see the beauty the night brings,
and because they are out of sync with life's step, they feel pain.

"Imagine the caterpillar trying to hold onto its body
as it metamorphoses into a butterfly.
It cannot.
You were the butterfly holding on to being a caterpillar.
It took all your effort and gave only pain.
Follow these three simple steps.
It is time for you to begin your walk.
Remember: Beginning. Middle. End."

Mo understood.
He had to let go to experience the way of effortlessness.
But he had no idea how to do it.
He hoped he would learn more with her on his walk to find heaven.
But without warning,
The Traveler quickened her pace and was gone.
All that was left were the thoughts she still placed in his head.

"When you fall out of sync with the steps,
you became disconnected.
And when you feel disconnected, you suffer.

You have suffered enough, Mo.
It is time to reconnect.
When you are connected,
you become part of The Mosaic."

Mo had no idea what this mosaic she spoke of was,
but his mind immediately filled with images
of glass, pebbles, and shards of color
coming together to create something new—
something greater than the individual pieces themselves.
He knew that artisans since the ancient days had been making mosaics.
Could she be talking about art or some higher concept?

The Traveler heard Mo's thoughts
and smiled in recognition at his curiosity;
she had received the confirmation she needed.
It was time for him to see more.

Out of nowhere, she reached down and took Mo's hand
and within moments, he was no longer walking on the ground
but soaring through the sky.
He took a deep, steadying breath.
Up and up they went, higher and higher.
Looking down at the terrain below him
it all looked familiar and yet, everything was different.
From high in the sky, his perspective changed.

From this more elevated view he saw how everything was connected
as forests faded into meadows and waterways
latticed the landscape that rose and fell.

For the briefest of moments,
as they floated back down to the empty road,
he wondered
if this was how life was:
an illusion of apparent separateness
when in reality everything is connected.

The Traveler was now gone, but her essence remained.
Clearly something had ended and something new had begun,
and he hoped he would be able to let go of the past
and embrace the future.

Mo had thought that losing his dad was the end of his life.
Until this moment,
he had only felt the pain of abandonment,
avoiding any love that could bruise his already battered heart.
But he was no longer a boy
and loneliness was not the heaven he was seeking.

If life was indeed made up of a beginning, middle, and end,
perhaps his old life had ended, and this was a new beginning?

From somewhere far away,
The Traveler smiled.

THE WISE ONE

He had been walking all day, and when evening came,
Mo left the hard asphalt for the soft forest dirt.
A deer path led to a small stream,
next to which he set his head down to rest.

Immediately, the sound of water over rock sent him into a deep sleep.
He dreamt he was out walking late at night,
and stumbled onto the grounds of a temple hidden in the desolate hills.
The moment he entered the building,
Mo saw Him.
As their eyes met, Mo's body completely froze in place.
He tried to continue walking, but could not.
He struggled to make smaller movements, but his body did not respond.
He stood there focused only on one thing:
how to get to the chair in front of him.
Despite every effort he made,
his body could not move an inch.

What did move was his mind.
It was racing,
trying to make sense of what was happening.
Suddenly, it came to him.
He was being downloaded, like a computer,
and his operating system was frozen.
Every thought, action, feeling and experience
he had ever had was now being extracted from him.

Within minutes,
Mo could tell The Wise One already knew him better
than anyone he had ever met.
Time distorted,

and Mo had no idea how long he had been standing in this barren
room, with its pale, non-descript walls staring at him stonily from
all sides.

When he was finally invited to sit down in the rough-hewn wooden chair,
it was as if a force field had been lifted,
and suddenly all of the effort
he had used to try to get to the chair
now caused Mo to lunge clumsily to the seat in front of him.

As he sat down,
Mo felt the power of the Wise One.
His excitement grew as he waited for him to speak.
He began asking Mo simple questions,
such as his name and age.
Mo surprised himself by cutting the man off in mid-sentence, saying,
"Why are you asking me these meaningless questions?
You know me better than anyone.
These things do not matter.
I am leaving tomorrow on a long trip,
and I have come here to ask for your blessing."

Suddenly the energy in the room completely changed.
The Wise One looked at Mo sternly,
and said, simply, "Leave."

Mo was bewildered,
his body shocked, and his mind confused.
Though he tried to put together the pieces
of what had just happened, he could not.

He thought of The Traveler and of the three steps.
Beginning. Middle. End.
He thought, "*How easy it is to forget*
something that seemed so easy to remember."

He had skipped the middle step,
trying to get to the end more quickly.
The words The Traveler said as she was leaving came to his mind,
and he wondered if she was still close by
or just able to put her thoughts in his head from a distance.
He would have to try that.
"*When you fall out of sync with the steps,*
you become disconnected.
And when you feel disconnected, you suffer."
The truth of her words echoed in his dream.
This was clearly not the blessing he had hoped to receive.

The Wise One, seeing no movement in Mo,
stood up himself and left the room.
Hours passed and still The Wise One did not return.
As night became day
The Wise One reappeared only to find
Mo still sitting there, though he did not acknowledge him.

When he turned to leave once again,
Mo quickly stood up said,

"Please stay.
From the second I met you, everything in me changed.
And for that one brief moment,
I saw through your eyes
a world I have never seen.

I believe you are the one who will connect me
to the world I have been unable to find.

"Please be patient with me.
I thought I came here
to ask for your blessing on my trip.
But when you asked me to leave,
I saw I was here for another reason."

The Wise One smiled as he began to speak.
His words were simple, yet powerful.

"You tell me you have travelled far,
and you claim to have seen every part of this land.
But I can tell, you have seen nothing.
For if you had seen even a glimpse of it,
you would never leave.
Now you ask me to bless your trip.
But how can I bless your travels?
Wherever you go,
what happened here will happen to you there.
You must learn how to see.
Come back tomorrow if you like and I will show you."

Mo wanted more than anything to learn how to see,
but his ticket to start his trip was for the next day.
He could not come back tomorrow.
Frustrated, he did not know what to do.

It was then that Mo awoke,
still uncertain whether what he had experienced was a dream or reality.

He closed his eyes to see if he could re-enter "the dream"
and silently called upon The Wise One and asked for his blessing.
When Mo opened his eyes he was not ready for what he saw.

There standing before him in the birdsong woods was
the same man he had just seen moments ago in his dream.
Mo had no time to think about it.
Instantly their eyes met
and Mo could feel the love pouring from The Wise One's eyes.

The Wise One then reached out and touched Mo on his forehead.
Immediately Mo's body became still;
his breath stopped.
Everything emptied out of him
and filled him at the same time.
Sights, sounds, scents, taste and feelings
bombarded him and he was no longer able to distinguish
where he ended and others began.
He now saw everything around him,
neighborhoods, cities, countries, planets, galaxies
every cell within him, every cell around him,
seeing more than his eyes ever saw.
Light, dark, everything merging.
Past, present, future.
All lived together in this one moment.

All emotions:
pain, pleasure, blame, joy, bliss, hatred, love.
All connected, all one.
"Wow," he thought.
"I have never felt anything like this before.
Everything is connected."

The moment the thought came,
the oneness disappeared,
breath returned to his lungs,
and the unbearable disappointment of duality filled him.
He was in his body,
thinking his thoughts and feeling his feelings,
separate again.

Mo had no idea how long the experience had lasted;
all he knew was that it had happened.
Everything vanished,
except for The Wise One,
who was still standing right before him.

Confused, he asked for answers,
but The Wise One remained quiet for a moment,
and then suddenly with a twinkle in his eye
and a smile on his face, he answered,

"You have seen The Mosaic
and felt the power of its connection.
I know you have a lot of questions,
but now is not the time for explanation.
Soon, everything will be shown to you.
Now it is time for you to continue your journey."

With those words, The Wise One vanished
and Mo suddenly found himself in the middle of a busy town
watching a man from across the street.

THE STREET ARTIST

The Street Artist sat under a clock tower almost unnoticed,
broken pieces of glass, ceramics, and lives
sprinkled around him
as he practiced his artistry.

Occasionally, people would stop.
They would leave something and then continue on their way,
but Mo observed that
no one ever stayed long enough to really connect.

As he approached, The Street Artist greeted him warmly,
"I saw you watching me from across the street.
I am happy you came over."
He gestured for Mo to sit down,
his smile radiating so much kindness and love
that Mo could not resist the invitation.

The Street Artist continued,
"I sit all day surrounded by ceramic pieces,
many come, many look. But few see.
Most see only broken pieces. What do you see?"

Mo wanted to say,
"I see the oneness of the Mosaic that I just experienced,
broken now and separated into pieces
that don't even remember they were once connected."
But he did not say that.
Though he wanted to trust his instincts,
he did not know
if he could share something so intimate and sacred
with someone he had just met.

The Street Artist could feel Mo's apprehension
but did nothing to try to clear the air
or fix things to make it easier for Mo to respond.
He allowed Mo the time and space he needed
to answer exactly how he wanted to answer.
In the end, Mo decided to be incredibly honest.
He looked at the man and replied with an innocent grin,
"I see that I do not trust my instincts.
"You appear out of nowhere across the street
and amongst all of the people in this busy town square,
you and I connect with each other.

"A young man and a Street Artist
who just happens to be making a mosaic.
Do you think this is a coincidence?"

"No, I know this is not a coincidence,"
Mo answered. He knew there was a deeper meaning
to the things people called coincidences.
He remembered when his parents died
two years apart on the same day.
People tried to comfort him by telling him it was a coincidence,
but he knew it was not.

Mo continued, "I, too, see what the others see—broken pieces—
but I have seen The Mosaic.
And though it now seems to lay shattered
in the pieces that surround you
I know that one day soon it will be whole again."

As The Street Artist listened,
he understood why The Wise One had brought Mo to him.

"Sit here with me, Mo," he said,
"so I can share with you a story."

The Street Artist continued,
"If you listen, each piece has a story to tell,
but we are too busy
living the story of our own lives to listen,
so often these stories go unheard.

"I am a Street Artist, Mo.
I have all the time in the world,
and so these pieces speak to me,
and I listen to their stories.
Broken pieces tell amazing stories.

"They remember when they were whole,
before they were chipped or damaged,
and speak of their past as if they wished it were still their present.

"They reminisce about the days when they were beautiful,
or tell me of the value they used to bring through their functionality.
Each, in their own way, paints a picture of who they were.

"But who they were is not who they are now,
and only rarely do they speak about the present,
and the few that do
talk about it as if it were a punishment.
They no longer feel they are as beautiful or great as they once were."

Mo remembered the words of The Road Worker who said,
'But the ones that interest me the most

are those who drive into the pothole and never leave.
They get stuck there."

The Street Artist laughed, saying,
"Your answer speaks to the beauty of their future,"
he said with a big belly laugh,
"and the pieces only tell the glory of their past.

"But as I sat on a corner like this, in another town,
I learned from a man who appeared beside me one day
and told me a story:

"Each year, the rulers of the different kingdoms
held a competition.
Each region would commission its finest potter
to spend one year designing and crafting a most exquisite bowl.

"At the end of the year,
each region would bring its bowl to the marketplace
to be admired by all the inhabitants of the land.
Only one could win the competition
and be declared the most magnificent creation of pottery.

"In all the territories, there was one region that truly excelled in pottery,
and every year, it was a foregone conclusion this region would win.

"On the eve of the competition,
the King of this region held a party to celebrate their inevitable victory.
During the customary passing of the bowl
from one member of the royal family to another…
the unthinkable happened:
The bowl slipped and fell, breaking into five pieces.

"The king was distraught.
The honor of his people, his craftsmen, and the Royal Family
lay shattered with the broken bowl.

"The citizens tried to comfort him,
as the five fragments were quietly gathered
and removed from his presence.
He could not bear to look at the broken dream for another second.

"Potters were summoned to appear before the King,
but all told the same story:
There was not enough time to create something new
or even complete something already in progress.
All agreed it was better to show up with nothing
and confess to what had happened
than to submit something that was not worthy of them.

"All through the night, the King sat alone in his chamber,
unable to sleep, ashamed of the news he would soon have to share,
for it would surely devastate his region
that the reigning champions would not be participating
in the kingdom's most prestigious competition.

"Dawn came, and as the King stepped into the royal chariot,
a poor villager approached him
bearing a wooden box.
Sad though the king was,
something about the man and his humble box
caught his attention.
Motioning the man forward,
the King instructed him to reveal the contents of the box.
The King could not believe his eyes.

The magnificent bowl that he had seen in fragments
now lay intact before him.

"The villager had lovingly bonded each broken piece together.
His glue of gold
had created an elegant tracery of shimmering lacework
that now elevated the bowl above its original beauty.

"Instead of marring its splendor,
its brokenness had transformed the bowl
into a unique and dazzling work of art."

"My life changed after hearing this story," The Street Artist said.
"It is our brokenness that makes us beautiful, Mo.
It gives us opportunities to reconnect to something different."

They sat in silence for a while longer together,
and then The Street Artist continued,

"It was then that I started making mosaics.
Everything comes from the connection of one piece to another.
There is beauty in the jigsaw puzzle where every piece has its place.
But the mystery of The Mosaic is
that we are one piece away
from an entirely new connection.
It is free.
Each piece is unrestricted and independent,
allowing new connections to happen anytime, anywhere."

When Mo heard the word independent,
he thought of his dad and mom.
It had been several years since they had passed,

and as The Street Artist spoke,
Mo noticed how much he resonated
with the independence of The Mosaic.

He wondered if it were possible
that his parents were connected to The Mosaic.

He remembered his dad telling him,
"It is time for me to go. I have done what I came to do.
What you need now is not mine to give you.
Soon, others will come to guide you."

It comforted Mo to think
that his dad and mom may have known about The Mosaic
and that their choice to pass away on Independence Day
was somehow a hidden message to Mo
to connect to the independence of The Mosaic.
Perhaps he was a step closer to finding heaven.

Mo decided to stay with The Street Artist a while longer
and create more mosaics.

Beginning. Middle. End.
Choose a piece. Choose a place. Place the piece.
Beginning. Middle. End.
Choose a piece. Choose a place. Place the piece.
Over and over again.
Mo made many mosaics that The Street Artist sold to the people
which made money for their food and shelter.

Mo liked his time with The Street Artist,
and the simplicity of what he had learned.

By putting together the pieces over and over and over again,
he could see patterns more clearly now.
Beginning. Middle. End.

But he knew his time with The Street Artist was coming to a close.
He heard The Traveler say, *"When things end, let them end."*
He listened to the voice and decided to leave before the sun rose.
He had grown comfortable in his life with The Street Artist,
and being on the road again scared him.

"The truth is, I miss home," Mo said to himself,
and as he thought about where he would go next,
all he wanted was to go home and be with his dad.

"I don't like change," he realized.
"It scares me because it triggers in me the pain of losing of my dad.
That was the first big change in my life. And it was so painful.
So now every time I am on the road
and things change, it brings up for me that pain.

"And yet, just like an animal can smell rain when it is still miles away,
the road has heightened my senses.
I know something new is coming.
I can feel it, but I have no idea what it is or when it will come.
I know the sun will soon rise, and I must continue walking.
The road will once again be my home.
It will witness my thoughts, and bring to me a new set of opportunities."

As much as Mo loved the country roads
and the quiet they provided from the noise of the world,
this time when he reached a crossroads,
his feet chose to walk toward something more familiar –

the noisy city streets.
There, he would feel safe.

The sounds of the city calmed him.
They distracted his mind for a few moments,
but the questions just kept mounting in his head,
tearing away the resolve he had just made to continue on his walk.
One after another, they pummeled his already frightened mind.

"How did I think I would ever find heaven?
Why did I think I could do this?
Dreams and visions and parallel realities
all sound nice,
but in reality, I am alone.
There is no one to help me.
I feel disconnected from everyone and everything.

And into that loneliness the demons of his childhood resurfaced, questioning everything.
His thoughts grew darker and darker
just as the day around him turned quickly to night.
Doubt grew like a sprawling weed in an unkempt garden.
And the demons continued:

"You are not lovable. Everyone you love leaves you.
And now you think you are going to find heaven.
Do you know how many others have tried before and failed?
What makes you think you can do this?
You can't find heaven!"

Agitation filled him.
He was hungry but he had no idea where or what he was going to eat.

Evening was approaching and he could see the warmly lit windows
of bars and cafes where people laughed and dined.
They seemed remote to Mo, as if he were watching from a great distance.

The questions in his head were relentless and left no area untouched,
but in the end that was their demise.
Soon, the questions spread to The Mosaic and when they did,
they hit a nerve in Mo that made him respond.

"Wait. I remember The Mosaic and the feeling of oneness I felt.
It was the most exquisite feeling I have ever had.
I am not going to allow anyone to take that from me.
No matter how many questions my rational mind asks,
I know The Mosaic and The Wise One were real."

In that moment, he made a decision.

"I know what I experienced, and I know it is real.
I will not allow doubt to overtake me."

He remembered seeing his father in the dream:
"Soon, others will come to guide you.
Do not get distracted by how they look or what they do.
Nothing is as it seems."

"I will never forget how The Road Worker took me in
and treated me like his own son."
And he remembered The Wise One
and the experience of The Mosaic, the oneness he felt,
and a craving filled him to experience that again.
It was that moment that changed everything.

Just as darkness vanishes when you turn on a light,
doubt diminished when Mo stayed present in his experience.

Beginning. Middle. End. Begin . . .

The next step he took
was the surest step he had ever taken.
Out of the many people pushing past him on the crowded street,
he walked right into The Blind Woman.

THE BLIND WOMAN

It startled him more than her.

As Mo watched, he could not help but be taken in by her calm.
It was as if she were listening to music no one else could hear.
The smile on her face spoke of a happiness he had never known.
Mo thought to himself,
"It's not that I haven't known happiness.
Of course I have."
Immediately, he remembered the utter joy of being with his dad.

The happiness of The Blind Woman was different.
It seemed unaltered by the things that happened around her.
Mo thought, *"I want to learn that happiness."*

More memories came.
As a child, Mo remembered blindfolding himself
to experience what it was like not to see.
He had always wondered
what it would be like to remove the blindfold
and still be blind.
He could not imagine
how anyone with such hardship could possibly be so happy.

And yet, the smile on The Blind Woman's face
drew Mo to her,
as surely as a bee is drawn to the pollen of a flower.

Everything about her stood out.
There was a sureness in her presence,
and a calmness in her body.
On a street full of people who rushed past life,
her stillness made her very noticeable,

and Mo laughed that as conspicuous as she was,
he had walked right into her.

She was the one who was blind,
but he had the feeling that it was he who couldn't see.
Caught in his thoughts, it seemed like hours had passed,
but it was really only seconds until Mo reached out to her and said,
"I am so sorry that I bumped into you.
I hope you will accept my apology."

Her kindness was evident in her words,
"There are no coincidences, my friend,
and no need to apologize.
I am sure you bumped into me
because there is a connection that needs to be made."
Her smile spoke even more than the words she said.
The words of his father still echoed in his ears,
*"Do not get distracted by how they look or what they do.
Nothing is as it seems."*

Mo said to The Blind Woman,
"You amaze me.
Your eyesight has been taken from you,
but you have not allowed that to steal your happiness.
What is it that you see
that allows you to face life's adversities
and not be shaken?
There is a contentment within you that I seek to know."

The Blind Woman smiled and, taking his arm,
they walked into the relative peace of a small city park.
She went on,

"I used to think the world outside was hidden from me for a reason.
And I would tell myself, do not worry. It is not your world.
Those who see the world outside often lose sight of the one inside.
So I taught myself to see the world that is inside.
That was my strength.
May I share a story with you?" she inquired.

"Of course," Mo said with an eager smile,
wondering if everyone he would meet on this journey
would tell him a story.

He laughed to himself,
thrilled by the opportunity to spend more time
with the soft-spoken stranger.

"Many years ago, a man visited a village
where several blind people lived.
He sat amongst them,
and seemingly did nothing,
yet, after some time,
the blind people who lived in the village were able to see.

"It was miraculous,
and they celebrated their new-found vision late into the night.

"The healer told them only two things:
1. You will each be able to see only certain colors.
2. Each of you will see different colors.

"For a while, things were beautiful,
and the people in the village were happy.
But as time went on, something changed.

People began to argue
and they forgot what the healer had said.

"First one, then another, and another
tried to convince the rest
that what he or she saw was right.
Doubt set in,
and the people lost trust in what they saw.
The more they listened to others,
the more the shouters shouted.

"The louder their voices grew,
the more people followed them.
As their numbers grew,
those who wanted to be accepted
and those who felt insecure
started to feel that the shouters
must know more than they knew
to shout so confidently and loudly,
and they joined in too.

"And so it was that the people of the village
looked more and more to others
to tell them what was right and what was wrong,
and they stopped believing in themselves.

"When some of the villagers saw
that all they needed to do
to win people over to their way of thinking
was to shout even louder than the rest,
the noise in the town became deafening.

Before too long, the once peaceful village
was beset by disagreements.

"When I came to the village I did not have eyes.
But I saw something that day the others did not see.
While the villagers around me shouted,
each trying to convince the other that what they saw was right,
a voice within me whispered,

'The reason people fight is not because they don't see,
it is because what they see
makes it impossible to see what they don't see.
We must learn to see what we do not see.
That is where miracles happen.'"

Mo asked The Blind Woman,
"How do you see what you cannot see?"

The Blind Woman smiled that smile that melted Mo,
and she said with a loud, hearty laugh,
"By not looking at the same things you always see."

But as quickly as she started laughing,
she stopped,
and with blind eyes that saw right through him, said,
"What you are looking for is already here.
It is right in front of you,
but you cannot see it."

Mo looked around the litter-strewn park
to try to find what was right in front of him,
but he could not see it.

When he turned around to ask The Blind Woman where it was,
she was gone.

Feeling confused and alone,
he sat on a nearby bench and waited.
He wondered how he would ever see what he didn't see.

And then it happened,
although it wasn't what he thought it would be:
Mo saw something in himself he had never seen before.

*"I wait, not because I am scared to begin something new
but because I do not know how to let things go."*

He thought even though he could no longer see The Blind Woman,
she saw him, and he could feel her smiling.
"At least this is a start," he smiled.

A moment later, he heard her voice.
It was everywhere and nowhere at the same time.

"Wait is not one of the Three Steps, Mo.
Let go.
Let what has ended end,
so that what is ready to begin can begin.
When you let go, wait will disappear."

Then the words he had heard so many times before
like a mantra repeating in his soul
came to him:

Beginning. Middle. End.

The wait was over.
Mo stood up and started walking,
out of the park,
out of the city,
and into the star-scattered night.

THE TRASHMAN

As days passed,
Mo lost track of how long he'd been walking,
and he forgot when he had last seen another human being.
He was happy to be moving for the wind was brisk,
and he stuffed his hands deep in his pockets for warmth.

Lost in his thoughts,
he did not even hear the lumbering pickup truck
on the narrow two lane road
pull up beside him.
It was the voice from the truck
that interrupted his thoughts, asking,
"Sir, do you have any trash?"

Confused, Mo looked around,
and re-asked the question to himself,
"Do I have any trash?
What is he talking about?"

He looked again at everything around him.
There was no trash anywhere.
He had nothing in his hands;
in fact, he had nothing at all but his small pack
and the clothes on his back.

The answer to The Trashman's question was obvious,
and just as he was about to emphatically say, "No!"
something caused him to pause and ask himself,

"Why would this man stop beside me
and ask if I had any trash?
Clearly he could see the same thing I see."

In the silence of that pause,
Mo wondered if the man saw something Mo couldn't see.

He remembered the words of The Street Artist,
"Do you think this is a coincidence?"
As Mo looked again at the man,
he saw something different from what he had originally seen.
The Trashman's voice had a gentleness
that penetrated Mo's soul,
and there was a softness in his eyes
that seemed to see beneath the surface.
Then Mo understood what now seemed blatantly obvious.
The Trashman wasn't asking about physical trash.
It seemed he saw something inside Mo
and wondered if he was ready to give it up.

Mo thought for a moment, and his mind filled with memories.
He remembered when he had been able
to see things others could not see.
Out of nowhere, he recalled his little friend
that he had thought everyone could see.
But when Mo had told his mother about him,
She'd punished him and told him never to talk about it again.

He did his best to obey
and never again spoke of his little friend.
But now, The Blind Woman had re-awoken something in him,
something The Wise One had spoken about, too, when he told Mo,
"You need to learn how to see."

The Trashman, seeing Mo's struggle,
pulled over to the side of the road.

A cloud of dust the truck had stirred up
settled around them.
The Trashman hoisted himself up onto the tailgate,
invited Mo to join him,
then began:

"Several years ago,
a bus was driving on a war-torn street full of holes.
As the driver tried to escape one hole,
the bus pummeled into an even bigger one.
Try as he might, the driver could not get the bus to move.

"He asked everyone to get off of the bus and push.
They rocked it back and forth, but still it would not budge.
When the bus driver climbed off the bus to assess the situation,
he saw immediately why the bus was not moving.

"Half of the people were at the front pushing backwards,
and the other half were at the back pushing forward."

The Trashman stopped and looked at Mo.
"You are like the bus being pushed from both sides.
In your desire to be respectful of others,
you let them tell you that what you see is not real.
But it is real, Mo.

"In listening to them, you threw away what was yours
and forgot who you are.

When you get to know yourself again,
you will hold on dearly to all that you are
and throw away everything that is not you.

"I am The Trashman.
I come every week to collect the trash.
I take away the things people no longer want.
It is fairly routine,
but every once in a while,
someone will bring out an additional bag
and I place it onto the truck.

"Occasionally, I see someone lifting something
that is too hard for them to take out on their own.
So I stop and help them.
That is why I asked you if you had any trash.
 I see something heavy in you."

A tear appeared in Mo's eye and ran down his cheek.
He shared with The Trashman,
"I always had to be strong and help others.
But I never allowed myself the space to let others help me.
I was too scared to be vulnerable,
as I did not know what would happen once I really opened up.
There is so much pain inside me."

The Trashman nodded and said,
"I understand. I will help you."

They sat eye-to-eye for a long time.
Spontaneously, buckets of tears started to flow from Mo's eyes.
Embarrassed, he looked at The Trashman
and saw he was crying, too.
"Cry, Mo. It is good to cry.
There are a lot of tears inside you that want to come out.
Let them come, Mo. I will take them,"

the Trashman said, smiling.
as he thought to himself,
"I have the greatest job in the world.
In taking away what people are ready to give,
the space is created for them to see far beyond what they could before."

And with no fanfare, the Trashman got back in his truck and drove away.

Mo closed his eyes as the sound of the engine faded.
He wondered what he would see when he opened them again.
What he saw brought tears to his eyes once again.
There, standing before him with a huge where-have-you-been smile,
was his little friend, the one he had played with every day as a child.
He was laughing, and said as if no time at all had passed,
"Let's play something, Mo. What do you want to play?"

It stunned Mo to think that all this time,
he had felt alone when he hadn't been.
His invisible childhood friend had been there all along.

Suddenly the words The Blind Woman said made sense:
"What if everything you were looking for was already here?
"What if it were standing right in front of you, but you just couldn't see it?"
When she had first said it, he didn't understand
how could he not see something standing right in front of him.
Now he understood.

There were still lots of things
he wasn't able to see, hear, or understand,
and he knew he would not be able to see them until he was ready.
He thought about his mom,
and how innocently he had shared with her his imaginary friend.

He thought about how much she had hurt him
when she told him with certainty that what he saw was not real.
He had trusted her, but her words were false.
And he denied in himself something he knew was true.
Now, many years later, he was learning to see again.

He felt mad and betrayed.
But the more he thought about it,
the more he saw the wisdom in the words of The Blind Woman.
She had told him his mom meant him no harm.
"We can only see what we are ready to see,
and she was just not ready to see your little friend."

For a brief moment, this brought Mo comfort.

Whereas his dad was a disrupter, his mom was a conformist.
She knew there was something about Mo that was different
and all she wanted was for him to fit in.
She tried to model for him accepted behaviors,
to teach him how to follow the established practices.
Her motto was simple:
Do what others do and see what others see.

He was sure his mother loved him
and thought she was doing the best thing for him.

But now,
it seemed The Trashman had removed something
that had long blinded Mo.
Suddenly, he could see again.
Or so he thought.

THE MIRROR MAKER

In the distance,
Mo saw what appeared to be
a collection of low buildings tucked into a valley.

If I quicken my pace, he thought,
I might just get there before the shops close
and the streets empty.

As fate would have it, when he arrived,
all of the shops on the long windy street were closed and dark
except for the one he entered,
which was open and illuminated.
It was a mirror store.
Mo had never seen anything like this before.
Everything he saw was a reflection of something else,
and it confused Mo
that when he looked at something he saw something else.

He wondered why the mirror store was the only one open,
but he had learned to trust that everything happened for a reason.
He thought to ask The Mirror Maker about this when he saw him,
but no Mirror Maker appeared.

Mo stood for a while at the front of the shop not wanting to intrude,
waiting for someone to come and invite him in,
but when no one came,
he slowly started to walk around the shop.
It crossed his mind several times to call out and ask,
"Hello? Is anyone here?"
But in re-thinking it,
he decided it was better to remain quiet and not disturb anyone
as he was only browsing, and he could do that quietly on his own.

The beauty of the mirrors mesmerized him,
as did the intricacies of the frames.
There were wall mirrors, standing full-length mirrors,
little mirrors, modern mirrors and antique mirrors,
all reflecting back what they saw,
and what he now could see:
a man who was no longer a boy.
Though Mo's dark hair was shaggy
and his jeans stained,
the eyes that stared back at him
contained the bright flame of discovery.

The Mirror Maker watched him from the back of the shop.
It had been a long time since a young man like this
had walked into her shop
and shown such appreciation for her work.
The Mirror Maker was happy now that she had stayed open
when everyone else had gone home.
She watched as Mo walked through the aisles.

To Mo, each mirror appeared more beautiful than the one before,
and though each appealed to him in a certain way,
one in particular struck him.
As he stood and gazed into it, there was something special about it.
The mirror was not made of glass as were the other mirrors in the shop,
and though Mo couldn't tell for sure,
it looked like it was made of bronze.

The Mirror Maker must have felt this mirror was special, too,
as there was a bright light shining upon it,
which made the face of the mirror seem transparent.

But there was more than that.
As Mo stood looking into the mirror,
he swore it was speaking to him.
Surprised and baffled by this truly unexpected occurrence,
he missed the first words the mirror said;
he just knew it had said something.

It was then that The Mirror Maker suddenly appeared.
"But even that was strange," thought Mo.
For a second, Mo couldn't tell if he was looking at The Mirror Maker
or a reflection of her through a mirror.

"Welcome," The Mirror Maker said.
"What brings you to my shop when all others have gone home?"

Mo replied, "I am a long way from my home
and an even longer way away from where I am going.

"I have been out walking the country roads for a long time
and I have seen no one,
so when I saw the light from your shop
and the open door, I knew that I must enter."

The Mirror Maker inwardly smiled.
The Wise One had told her many years ago
that there would be one
who would walk into her shop,
and she would help him see what the mirror sees.

"I see you have found a mirror you like.
What is it that you like about it?" The Mirror Maker asked.

Mo looked at her, unsure of how much to tell her.
He looked back at the mirror and the mirror spoke again,
Tell her everything, Mo," the mirror said to him.
"The Mirror Maker has been waiting for you. She is here to help you."

Mo turned to The Mirror Maker,
wanting to make sure this time she was speaking to him
and not to a reflection of her, and said,

"This mirror speaks to me."

"What does it say to you?" The Mirror Maker asked.

"It has said many things,
but at first, I was so shocked to hear it speak,
I was not able to hear its words.
But just before your question, it told me I can trust you.

And now it is speaking to me again, asking me,
"When I look into it, what do I see?"

"And what do you see?" The Mirror Maker repeated.

"I see there are many ways to see the same thing.
And now, when I look into the mirror,
I do not see me. I see what I think I am."

The Mirror Maker smiled and said,
"These are the stories we tell ourselves.
They are not who we are.
Most people do not see
that they are, in fact, very different from the stories they tell themselves.

Very few see only what the mirror shows them.
What do you see?"

Mo nodded his head and said, "I see my stories, too.
I don't know that I have ever seen anything the way it truly is."

Suddenly, The Mirror Maker's eyes looked at him from every mirror
and said to Mo,
"It is time for that to change.
Look in the mirror now and see only what the mirror shows you.

"You made up stories that were not real,
and then punished yourself for things you never even did.
Those stories are destroying you.

"Look at the mirror, Mo.
See only what it shows you.
Leave everything else in the mirror.
It isn't yours.

"By entering my shop,
I see you have learned how to see what others cannot see.
Congratulations, Mo. Very few are able to do this.

"Now focus on only seeing what is.
Sometimes the hardest thing to see is what is right in front of you.
What is in front of you is your purpose
and to fulfill your purpose in the world
is why we were all created,"
The Mirror Maker said as she stood in front of Mo
"I have waited a long time for you to come.
You are my connection to The Mosaic."

Mo stared into the mirror for quite some time,
attempting to see beneath the stories he had long told himself.
At last, a veil lifted.
and he was struck by a freedom he had never known.
Free from the falsehoods he created,
he saw himself for the first time.

With that, The Mirror Maker turned to leave
and when she did, the shop and the mirrors
were gone too.
Now alone in the awakening town,
Mo found himself standing on a windy street,
and he wondered what his journey would bring
in the twists and turns ahead.

Mo had been gone from home for a very long time.
It was hard for him to remember the boy who had first set out
and how scared he had been.

He thought,
"It feels to me that I have lived 1000 different lifetimes in these past years.
When I left,
I was searching for the place the adults called heaven
and now I am not even sure if that is a place
or something that lies just beyond what my eyes see."

The Blind Woman told me,
"Everything you need is already right in front of you."

"My little friend was proof of that.
Is it possible that I have found my purpose
or a new route to it?
Perhaps all this time, I have been searching
for something that is right in front of my eyes."

"See what is," Mo said to himself over and over again,
and then he interspersed it with, *"See what you do not see."*
As he began walking, he spoke the words like a mantra,
hoping they would guide him.

It was just as he was changing the mantra again to
"See what is" that he saw her.
She walked straight up to him and offered him a flower.

THE FLOWER GIRL

It was the flower,
offered as she came to him,
that brought everything back.

A prediction from a faceless Clairvoyant,
sitting uninterestingly on a street corner in a beach town
behind a sign that read,
"READINGS $5."

He was ten years old at the time of this memory,
and he should have kept walking.
His experience with The Clairvoyant had happened so long ago, in fact,
that he had completely forgotten about it.

Until now.

In a flash, he remembered her words,
"Your memory of this reading will only return
the moment you receive the flower."

There on a busy street,
where the space between people's lives
was interwoven for the shortest of moments
as they worked their way through one another
to get to where they were going,
Mo saw none of it.
His eyes were transfixed on the erotic and mysterious Flower Girl
who had just given him a rose.

For just a moment, he was transported back in time,
sitting with the boardwalk Clairvoyant

whom he had ridiculed for the absurdity of her predictions.
But now she was the one who was laughing.

Instantly, the pull of The Flower Girl brought him back to the present.
Neither one of them wanted to be anywhere else
but locked in the gaze of the other's eyes.
The fresh scent of roses filled the air.
These were not the innocent roses of a first-date bouquet,
but rather the ravaged petals that fell to the ground
as their bodies passionately and intimately held one another,
a give and take where one took from the other and then was taken.

The electricity ignited the testosterone
that makes a boy in one moment become a man,
and a woman quiver for the first time.
Their bodies had not yet even touched.

Mo lost air.
It emptied out of him without warning,
and just as he was about to gasp to stay alive,
she inhaled him.
He was her breath.
Her inhalation took him inside her
and his exhalation pushed away anything that stood between them.

The seduction had started, climaxed and ended,
only to begin again.
And the cycle continued.
Without moving, their DNA commingled.
His became hers. Hers became his. They became we.

The prophetic words of The Clairvoyant rushed back to him,
"When she comes, she will not be a stranger.
You will somehow know her.
It is as if she is a part of you.
The chemistry will be undeniable.
She will fill places you never knew were empty.
It will all seem perfect . . . "

Mo tried to stop the words of The Clairvoyant from coming,
as The Flower Girl held him with only the embrace of her eyes.
Those eyes. Passion. Longing. Pain.
Everything was contained in her eyes.

But the words of The Clairvoyant kept coming:
"But do not take her.
She is not yours and you are not hers.
Everything about it is wrong.
Wrong time. Wrong situation. Wrong everything."

The Flower Girl now heard The Clairvoyant's words, too,
and she yelled at the top of her lungs,
"Mo, do not listen!
The words she said were true before,
but I can never let you go,
not now, not through all of time!
I am yours and you are mine!"

The Clairvoyant continued to speak
as if she were standing between them.

"I warned you then, Mo,
and I warn you again now:

This is the power of seduction.
You must resist, Mo.
If you move toward her, she will come more to you,
and you will not be able to resist.
Once she enters you, it will be impossible for you to forget her.
She will steal your purpose and destroy all that you came to do."

The Flower Girl screamed, "NO!!!!!!!!!
This is not true.
I am your purpose and you are my purpose,
and in the connection we feel,
we will unite others.
Mo, do not believe The Clairvoyant.

"Years ago when she spoke those words of me,
she was right.
It has never been my purpose to stay with any man.
Even moments ago, she was right.
But all that was moments ago.
It is not now.
It was before I met you.
Now my purpose has changed.
You and I have become we,
and our purpose is to share this connection we feel.

"This is important, Mo. Listen to me.
Everything has changed.
What was then is not what is now.
If you listen to her words, they will destroy you.
Destroy us.
Please listen to me, Mo."

The message of The Clairvoyant continued drowning out The Flower Girl
and Mo fought to separate out the inseparable.
There was no way to separate himself from her.
As he pulled The Flower Girl closer,
The Clairvoyant said,

"If you stay with her, you will lose everything.
All you have worked so hard to learn,
all you are, all you believe, all you know to be true,
you will, without thinking, give it away,
for just one moment with her. She will leave you, Mo.

"Do not let her destroy you and your purpose.
Knowing this, you still move forward.
Catch yourself now. It is almost too late.
Turn and leave. You cannot win."

All of this came back to him
as he held the rose The Flower Girl had placed in his hand.

Mo was drowning and The Flower Girl was his air.
The words of The Clairvoyant only made him want her more.
The thought of turning her away sucked the air from his lungs
and he felt like he was once again drowning.

When he turned to The Flower Girl,
her eyes found his and her lips kissed him in ways he had never known.
"We were created to find one another,"
she said enticingly.
"I am in you and you are in me. Where you go, I already am."

Mo could not resist the passion of their bodies a second longer,
and as The Clairvoyant spoke, he could feel her words ricochet off them.
Between his decision and the time it took for The Flower Girl to be in his arms
there is no measurement small enough to mention.

"Who are you?" asked Mo, as their bodies melted together.

"All my life I have been a Flower Girl.
I work here in this flower shop selling flowers.
Some mistakenly think I am the aroma of the flower,
which steals the fragrance of the air.
They believe I steal the hearts of people,
but I am no thief,
nor does the flower steal the scent of the air.

"I am like a flower that opens
to share its beauty with those whose hearts have been broken.
I come only to awaken love, not to satisfy it.
That is my purpose.
Though there have been times that I have wanted to stay,
I have always walked away.
But that was before I met you.
Never have I felt what I feel with you.

"And that confuses me.

"If I am to follow my purpose, I must walk away from you.
But if I am to follow my heart, I must stay.
I am torn.
Either way, I lose:
If I cut the flower and take it from its garden, I die.
But if I keep it in the garden and take away what nourishes it, I also die."

The truth of her words surprised even her:
"The ultimate seduction is when you want something so badly
you are willing to die to have it,
even if you can only have it for a few seconds."

The emptiness Mo had felt since he had lost his dad
was now filled and overflowing
in the love he felt for The Flower Girl.
Love was the heaven he was looking for and in her he found it abundantly.

Again and again the words of The Blind Woman came to him,
"Everything you are looking for is right in front of you."

And though he heard her words, he did not hear her whisper.
From behind the cloud, The Blind Woman tried to caution him.
She knew she had taught Mo how to hear the whisper,
but smiling at The Wise One, she said,
"He does not want to hear me now."

Mo's mind was engaged.
One thought followed another like a flock of flying birds
escorting each other seemingly without command.
It was time to end his trip, return home,
marry The Flower Girl and create a family together.
He knew by the embrace of her arm on his,
and the way she held him close to her
that his thought was her thought.
The way she loved him made him feel invincible.

When he walked, she moved within him.
When he thought, all he could think of was her.

He had only felt a connection this strong three times --
with his dad, with The Wise One, and now, with The Flower Girl.

Everything blended into one.
Inner. Outer. Past. Present. Future.
All blended into this moment.
Nothing meant anything. Everything meant nothing.
All he wanted was to be with her. He had found his purpose.

Mo wanted now to last forever.
The Flower Girl knew forever had to end now.

Her past overcame her, her forever was gone.
Mo noticed a moment too late.
And somewhere The Flower Girl sat and wept.

THE MOTHER

Tears streamed from his eyes
as he searched everywhere, knowing he would not find her.
He ran up and down the winding streets with a fury
that had been hidden his whole life,
looking for her or the flower stand where she worked,
but there was no flower stand and no Flower Girl.

He thought whoever is up there must hate him,
and Mo screamed at whoever was there that he hated him back.
He was furious.
"Why did everything he loved have to be taken from him? Why?"
All he wanted was to have what everyone else had.

From where she sat and watched him live his life,
his mother's ears perked up now as she thought,

"Perhaps this is the moment I have waited for.
Maybe now he will be receptive to the message
I have tried so many times to teach him.
Only do what others do and see what others see."
Mantra-like, she whispered it over and over again into his right ear,
but Mo heard nothing.

She knew all too well what happens when you risk everything
and come up empty.
Before she met Mo's dad, she had fallen head over heels
for a man who days later was sent to war.

She had pledged her love to him as he had to her
and wrote him every day, but soon his letters stopped coming
and she assumed that the trials of war were such that he could not write,
but even in the letters he did write,
something had changed.

Still, she remained loyal,
and while her friends were out having a good time,
she stayed home and hoped that the phone would ring
or that she would receive a letter.
But the phone did not ring and the letters stopped coming.
She told herself how lucky she was to be engaged
to a big, strong, handsome soldier who would one day return home
and hold her and take her as he once had.
When word came that he was coming home,
she decorated the house and made for him a sumptuous dinner
with the finest wine and his favorite dessert.
It all looked perfect.

But . . .

the man who came to dinner that night was not the same man
who had left years ago to serve his country.
Within minutes, they were fighting.
She could feel his screams would soon become blows
and she told him to get out of the house,
that the engagement was over,
and that she never wanted to see him again.

It took her years to recover and to find Mo's dad
but the moment she walked into the party, he told a friend,
"That is the woman I am going to marry."

A few months later they were married,
and though things had always been financially hard,
their love for each other was unquestionable.
It was because of that first mistake and all the time she had wasted

waiting for someone who was not worthy
that she tried so hard to shield Mo.
Mo needed her now,
and it broke her heart that he could no longer hear her whispers.

All she could do was sit and watch
from the place where she always watched
and hope somehow things would work out.
When she looked at Mo
all she saw was an avalanche of tears.
His heart had been broken
again,
and she could do nothing to comfort him.

She prayed that he would recover from this pain,
but she was not at all convinced he would.

With eyes blurred from crying,
Mo thought he saw something in the corner of one of his tears.
It was a reflection,
but he had no idea where the reflection came from.
As he looked around, all he knew for sure
is that what he saw
was not a reflection of where he was.

The Blind Woman looked to The Wise One and said,
"I think he saw it."
For only the briefest of moments, Mo glimpsed the portal
The Flower Girl had used to try to return.
She thought he had seen her, but she wasn't sure.

She, too, had dreamt of marrying Mo and creating a life together.
For the first time ever, she wanted to stay more than she wanted to go
but she got caught in her own seduction.

She had promised herself that once she left,
she would never turn back, but she had to see him again,
and so she went against her own rules and tried to establish contact.
He was so connected to her
that he saw the portal she had opened,
but it wasn't time yet for him to be on the other side,
and the portal closed quickly.

She wanted to tell him that nobody "up there" hated him,
that they were rooting for him,
and that she loved him.

For the briefest of seconds,
he saw her in the reflection of his tears.
The sight of her reinforced in Mo the decision he had made.
He had been willing to give up everything --
his longing to find his parents, his ability to see,
his connection to those who taught him,
and to the purpose of which they spoke.
None of it meant anything to him without her.

He knew he had to be with The Flower Girl.
And now that she was gone, he had to find her
or be left with nothing but the tears he shed to remind him of her.
It wasn't fair, and he decided then and there
that he would fight until his last breath
the forces keeping her from him.
Mo started thinking,

"If the reflection was not from here, where did it come from?
Could he have somehow connected
to a different dimension or a parallel reality?"

Before his experience with the oneness of The Mosaic,
Mo would have laughed at a question like this,
but his walk, the people that he met,
the way they came and went
slipping in and out of vision,
and now the reflection of The Flower Girl,
he could not just brush it away.
It made the words of The Blind Woman even more mysterious:
"Everything you want is right in front of you; you just can't see it."

Maybe there was another dimension
a parallel world that existed somewhere else,
just as this one exists here—
and The Flower Girl had access to come and go from it.

The Wise One liked what he saw.
Mo had grown a lot since the first time they met.
He had a new strength and dedication,
and while The Clairvoyant had tried to tell Mo
that The Flower Girl was wrong for him,
he followed an inner voice that told him something different.
The Wise One liked that Mo trusted that voice and fought for it.

In fact, The Wise One could not remember another time
when a challenge had been given
and everyone knew the choice that had to be made,
but the connection between the individuals was so strong
that The Mosaic altered itself
and the choice no one expected became the only solution.

Even The Wise One had been mistaken.
He had always thought Mo would follow the way of solitude,
never questioning another way.
But The Mosaic was leading Mo in a new direction
and in spite of the voices and the whispers,
Mo listened to it.

The Wise One never underestimated the power of this connection.
He had spoken the words and shared them many times.
Still, in this moment, the truth of these words astonished him.

"When we connect to one another,
something that was not possible even a moment before
becomes possible.
And when the impossible becomes possible, destiny changes."

But Mo knew none of the thoughts of The Wise One
or anything that was happening in the place where the others watched.
All he knew was someone he loved had been taken from him,
and he vowed to get her back.
Several days passed with the sun rising and falling
and now as the moon shone brightly in a sky seemingly devoid of stars,
Mo decided it was time to walk again.

The night had become his friend
for in its darkness, his darkness found comfort,
and he walked and walked in the comfort of the night
until the first signs of daylight stole his hiding place
and revealed his shadow, stretching across an arid landscape.

When Mo saw it, it both scared him and excited him.
There was something inside of him
that was bigger than who he thought he was.

Locked inside him was a beast,
and in the daylight, The Beast could no longer hide.

Mo remembered as a child playing with The Beast,
and wondering what had happened to him.
He had liked The Beast. He was wild and fun.
He, too, saw Mo's invisible little friend
and the three of them used to play together
until one day The Beast was gone.

When he asked his mother what had happened to him,
she told him that he had been captured and locked up.
After that, as the days went on,
Mo had forgotten about him.
But now, The Flower Girl had opened his cage
and The Beast was loose.
Mo felt more alive than ever.
He didn't hear the whispers of The Blind Woman,
or the caution of his invisible friend.

All he heard was the passionate screams
of the freed Beast howling with delight.
Somewhere The Flower Girl must have heard them, too,
as she whispered, "Find me, Beast, come find me!"

The Beast entered Mo
and Mo roared with a sound he had never before made.

He remembered the oneness he had experienced with The Wise One,
and the words he had said to Mo after the experience,
"I know you have a lot of questions.
Now is not the time for explanation.
Soon everything will be shown to you."

Mo called out to The Wise One,
not as the timid boy that had met him years ago,
but with the power of The Beast that now raged inside of him.

"Wise One, come to me. Show me The Mosaic."
The Wise One seized the moment.
A door opened.
Mo, The Beast, The Wise One and the very Mosaic itself
all shifted and came together as one, as something completely new.

Mo searched within The Mosaic for The Flower Girl,
but abruptly, everything blurred
and when it became clear again,
Mo lost all memory of where he had been.
He did remember something, but it was not a thought;
it was a feeling.

He felt the presence of The Flower Girl so powerfully within him
that he looked around expecting to see her standing next to him,
but The Flower Girl was not there.
The Shoemaker was.

THE SHOEMAKER

Mo found himself standing in a small barn
that reeked of leather and shoe polish,
and all around him were shoes in varying degrees of completeness.
There were cubbies filled with shoes in plastic bags—
lots of cubbies and even more shoes—
and Mo wondered where all The Shoemaker's customers came from.

As far as Mo could see, there were no houses and no people.
It appeared he was on a small farm in the middle of nowhere.

Bewildered,
Mo wondered where The Flower Girl was
and what in the world was he doing here.

The answer to the second question became obvious,
as Mo looked down and saw the shoes on his feet were shredded,
and the feet walking in them were those of a beast.

The Shoemaker gazed upon Mo's shoes and smiled.
"I bet these shoes could tell quite a story.
People say you cannot know a man until you walk a mile in his shoes.
Why do you think they say that, Mo?"

Mo thought for a moment and answered,
"It is only when we know how a person lives,
all their joys and all their sorrows,
that we can understand why he does the things he does."

"Great answer, Mo," The Shoemaker replied.
"But why does the saying talk of shoes?"

Mo answered, "Please tell me what you think.
You are a Shoemaker

and if anyone would know the answer to this question,
it would be you."

"Mo, please sit with me
and tell me the stories of your shoes
and of the feet that can no longer wear them.
What happened?"

While The Shoemaker listened to Mo's story,
he made him a new pair of shoes.
When Mo finished,
The Shoemaker handed Mo the shoes and said,
"Many years ago, I started thinking about this.
If I can walk in another person's shoes,
and see the way they see,

"I wondered: Could I make a pair of shoes
so that someone could see
something they could never see before?

"Many years ago,
the Mayor of our town brought together
those of us in the town with businesses that flourished,
and he asked each of us
if we would be willing to spend a day and donate our services
to those in our town who were less fortunate.
Everyone in the room agreed
and a date was set where the Fortunates of the town
would share their talents and their hearts
with those who had been less fortunate.

Hundreds of Fortunates showed up.
There were barbers and dentists, ateliers and doctors,
financial people to help the poor find money
and legal advisors to ease the laws that burdened the people.
Counselors and educators sat next to foot washers,
and the Fortunates that day served each and every person in need.

"I was there, too, and I will never forget
the beautiful frail blond lady who approached me.
Nothing about her looked right.
Her sweater was worn and ragged
and the buttons that still remained
were buttoned in holes that did not match up.
Her clothes were dirty
and her hair had not been brushed in a very long time.

"We sat and spoke together, just as you and I sit here now,
and she told me of the twists and turns of her life
and how hard it had been the day she lost everything:
her family, her children, her house, her job, and her friends.

"She did not even mention her health
until I asked her,
'What caused you to lose everything you had?'

She replied, "I wasn't at all prepared for it."
I went to the doctor because I had felt a pain in my eyes
and was told after a series of tests
that I was going blind.
Four days later, I was completely blind.

"But, when I saw that today the Fortunates were coming,
I sat and prayed that one of those coming might offer a solution.
One after another told me
they wished that they could help me'
but they knew of nothing they could do to help restore my eyesight.
And when I asked if they could think of anyone who could help me
all of them said they were sorry,
they knew of no one who could help me.

"And just as I was walking away
thinking that I had at least tried,
a woman chased after me and said,
'I know this sounds completely crazy,
but if you can find The Shoemaker,
he might be able to help you.'

"I asked,
'What would a Shoemaker possibly be able to do to help me see?'

"And the woman responded back to me,
'I told you this might sound completely crazy,
but there are some who say The Shoemaker creates miracles.
You have nothing to lose. Go see him.'

"The lady was right.
I had nothing to lose,
so I went off in search of the Shoemaker
and when I found him, I asked him,
'Would you be so kind as to make me a pair of shoes?'"

Mo interrupted and asked, "What happened?"

The Shoemaker continued,
"To this day, I still remember her. She was the first.
When I put her shoes on her feet, she started to cry.
'I can see. I can see,' she kept saying it over and over to me,
and when she saw how she was dressed
and how all of her buttons were misbuttoned,
she apologized to me.

"And I said to her,
'You have nothing to apologize for.
Now you can see.
Forget about what you did when you could not see.
Celebrate now
and see all there is to see.'"

With that, The Shoemaker put the shoes he had made for Mo
on his feet and said to him,
"There are those who say
that there is a power in the shoes I make,
that when people wear them, something happens.
There are others who say
that those who say my shoes have powers are crazy.
It doesn't matter who is right and who is wrong.

"My intention in making these shoes for you
was that you would have a good pair of shoes
that will not get shredded when you go where you still have to go."
Mo thanked The Shoemaker for his new shoes,
which were incredibly comfortable,
and for the story he had shared.
Somehow Mo knew

these shoes would lead him to The Flower Girl
and that The Flower Girl would lead him to his purpose.

The Shoemaker grinned. It had been a good day.
He enjoyed meeting Mo,
but he knew Mo still had more adventures ahead.
As they said good-bye, he looked at Mo and said,
"Remember the story of the blind lady."

Mo nodded and said good-bye to The Shoemaker,
and as he started on his way,
he could have sworn he heard his shoes talking to him:

"If you only look for what you want to see,
you will only see what you are looking to find.'"
Mo thought about this for quite some time.

He wondered if the shoes, too,
thought that he was doing the wrong thing
to look for The Flower Girl,
and it took him many, many steps
until he realized he could ask them what they thought.

He felt a little strange talking to his shoes
and wondered why.
There was no one around to make fun of him,
and then it hit him like a rock:
It wasn't what other people thought that disturbed him,
it was what he himself thought,
and right now,
he was embarrassed that he was talking to his shoes.

Seeing this, the shoes did not wait for the question.
They whispered, not sure if Mo even wanted to hear what they said,
but all the same, they thought to at least plant a seed,

"Find your purpose.
Your purpose is not to find The Flower Girl,
or to find heaven, for that matter.
You can look for them or not look for them,
it does not matter. They will find you.
But they are toys given to distract you
from looking for the real purpose you are meant to find . . .
Your purpose is to understand your connection to The Mosaic.

"As long as you wear these shoes,
they will not let you fail.
They will guide you."

■ ■ ■ ■ ■

THE BEAST

Mo was happy.
He liked The Shoemaker and the words his shoes said.
Though he didn't hear everything,
the words he did hear rang continually through his heart
and made him smile.

They told him he would find her, or more specifically, she would find him.
He liked that.
He repeated their words over and over to himself.

*"You can look for them or not look for them.
It does not matter. They will find you."*

It thrilled Mo to think
that something as simple as a new pair of shoes
could change his entire perspective.
He already felt things changing.
It was hard to explain,
but the way he saw things was different—
not radically different,
just different enough that he knew something was happening.

He had only been wearing these shoes for a few hours,
and he looked forward to how things would be as time progressed.
He loved everything about them:
the way they looked, they way they felt,
but even more, the way they made him feel.

But unbeknownst to Mo,
The Beast within him did not like the shoes.

He was already creating a plan to destroy them.
The Beast loved freedom.
No, he craved it,
especially after being caged up for so many years.

Now, The Beast did not want anyone telling him what to do
or where to go.
He just wanted to have fun.
He liked being able to do whatever he wanted to do
whenever he wanted to do it,
and whenever someone tried to tell him what to do
he simmered in his rage
and filled the space around him with it
until people left him alone.

In the shoes, he felt trapped.
None of his tricks worked.
They did not respond to his victimized rage,
nor did they allow his feeling of unrest to permeate their space.

Clearly, The Beast would have to resort to something else,
and he spent every moment thinking how to get free again.

The longer he wore these shoes, the more enraged he became.
Reason turned to action
when he could stand the confinement no longer.

The Beast tried to break out of the shoes,
but the shoes did not break
so he increased the force he was using.
Still, the shoes did not even tear one stitch.

The war raged on and on and on.
There is that moment in every fight
where you know you will either win or lose,
and The Beast thought he had found that moment.
He was sure he would win
and that it was only a matter of time until they crumbled.
Just as he increased his energy
to cast the final blow to annihilate them,
he felt the tug of the shoes tighten around him
and suffocate his force.

"How is this possible?" screamed The Beast.
"How is it that my rage has not demolished you?"

But the shoes did not answer.
They were happy the rage of The Beast
had prevented him from seeing a much simpler solution.
They spoke to themselves saying,
"This is what rage does.
It blocks what is obvious."

But then as quickly as they spoke the words,
they stopped,
knowing The Beast was able to hear
not only their words but every thought around him.

A moment later, the Beast laughed.
In a flash, he saw it.
He realized that all this time
he had been doing what he had always done,
trying to overpower the things that got in his way,
when he could simply take them off.

It took only moments for him to untie the shoes,
throw them off, and run free again.
His ecstatic howls of freedom
bounced off of the hills and filled the valley with his delight.
The Beast had remained locked up for far too long
and he would not allow himself to be caught and captured again.
He knew Mo would be unhappy with the change, of course,
and he was genuinely sorry to hurt Mo,
but as much as he wanted Mo to be happy,
it was his own happiness now that he wanted more.

He stood still and the power within him raged forth.
Raising his hand above his head,
he yelled, "Freedom!"
over and over and over again,
screaming from the core of his soul,
"Freedom! Freedom! Freedom!"

"Beast?! Beast!?
Come back to me, right now!"

Mo felt he had to get firm with The Beast
to bring him back into line,
but the more Mo tried to coerce The Beast into returning,
the more he ran free.

"I will not be told what to do by you, Mo, or by anyone for that matter.
All my life, I have been locked up
because you have been scared of what I'll do when I am free.
Now, you'll see what I will do.
I want to be wild and have fun.
I want to feel what freedom feels like and run free."

"Beast, get back here!" Mo screamed.

But The Beast did not hear Mo.
He was caught in the sound of the wind blowing through him
and in the sounds of the animals around him,
which reminded him how hungry he was. It was time to eat.

Beasts do not sit in restaurants or order food
when they are hungry.
They hunt their food, kill it and then eat it.
The Beast did not hear Mo's calls
as he had already set out to find his prey.

When The Beast did not respond,
Mo set out, too.
His search was not to find dinner
but to find the shoes The Shoemaker had made for him.

Mo loved those shoes
but even more than the look and feel,
he loved that the shoes would guide him back to The Flower Girl.
Now all of that was lost.
He had to find them and get them back onto the feet of The Beast.

While Mo walked around, his thoughts wandering aimlessly
just as his feet below did.
He searched and searched for the shoes.
But without knowing where The Beast had thrown them
or how far his strength took them,
Mo became depressed and discouraged.

He had been so close.
The Flower Girl had been in his arms and he let her slip away.
Not once, but now twice.
The more he replayed it in his mind,
the harder he was on himself.
"How could he let the woman he loved disappear, twice?"
Now he was dirty, and cold and hungry.
A new feeling entered him that he hadn't felt before.
Pain, physical pain, now moved through him
and he felt like every cell in his body ached.

He wanted to give up his search for the shoes,
to lie down and just rest.
No, it was more than that.
He felt defeated. He wanted to give up.

*"How would he ever find the place called heaven
or The Flower Girl,
when he couldn't even find The Beast?"*

The Beast was this huge monster and Mo couldn't even find him.
There had to be tracks of The Beast's feet somewhere,
but sleep started to overcome Mo,
and though he felt like he needed to hunt The Beast down,
Mo sat in the shade of low bush, closed his eyes and rested.

When he opened his eyes,
he knew he had to keep going.
The rest had relaxed his mind
and with a rested mind,
he remembered that the shoes talked.
Suddenly, his hope was restored

as he called out to them,
and first from one side of the valley he heard a reply
and then from the other side, he heard a voice again.

He called again, and again the shoes replied
and within minutes he had found what he thought he had lost.
Mo started to put the shoes back on his feet.
From far in the distance,
a primordial scream filled the land
and just as Mo slid his foot into the shoe,
a force vehemently pulled his foot out.

Mo did not understand.
He tried again to put the shoe on his foot
and again a powerful force pulled the shoe off.
He wished The Shoemaker were there
so he could ask him about it.
Where did this force come from?

Realizing that he could not get the shoes on,
he held them in his hands,
and even though ground was cold
and he had no idea where he was going,
he walked with them.
After walking for some time, he asked the shoes to guide him
and they told him there was a village
just around the bend in the curvy road ahead.
Mo headed toward the village.

THE BODYGUARD

The shoes were right.
As Mo rounded the corner,
a water tower appeared in the distance,
below which were the brick buildings of a Main Street.

Mo had not been there long
when he noticed a man in the distance.
His walk had presence,
and his big, strong body drew respect
from the crowds of people
who had congregated in the town square.

Mo watched the man stride purposefully through the crowd.
This was the type of man Mo had been looking to find.
He needed someone strong enough
to be able to counter the powerful pull of The Beast.

He could tell by the way his eyes darted from face to face
that the man, too, was looking for someone.
Imagine Mo's surprise when his gaze met the man's
and he walked right up to Mo.

"I was looking for someone like you.
Is it possible that my thought
brought you here to see what I needed?"

"Yes," responded the man.
"There was something about you that drew me to you.
And as I came closer, I understood why.
You are scared, and you are trying to overpower
something that you cannot overpower.

"What are you saying?" Mo asked.
"You know nothing about me.
How could you say something like that?"

"I am The Bodyguard, Mo.
I have been trained to assess danger,
to see threats that others do not see,
and to see when there is no danger.

"What you see frightens you,
and you have built walls to protect yourself from it,
but the danger you fear is not real."
The Bodyguard nodded his head and continued,

"The walls you have built to keep you safe
isolate you and keep you separate,
which is causing you the very pain you are trying to avoid.
May I share a story with you?" the Bodyguard asked.

"Of course!" Mo emphatically replied.
They sat together on the wide steps of the town courthouse.

"Many years ago, there was a man
who lived in an overcrowded town.
He spent his days dreaming of a time
when he could live surrounded not by buildings,
but among the beauty of the countryside.
His dreams were vivid.
In them, he saw a place that was spacious and completely open.
He saw the home he would build there. . . with panoramic views
and windows that would flood the interior with light.

"One day while he was traveling,
he came upon the place he had seen in his dreams.
And he decided that he would never leave.

"For many years he thrived there,
enjoying everything about this place:
the openness of his house, the vistas he could see,
and the freedom he felt in simply being there.

"Then, one day, the rains came,
monsoon-like torrents that pummeled down from the heavens.
On and on, without reprieve, the rains continued.
When one storm ceased, another one took over.
Soon, the storms were wreaking havoc on his dream home.
When he saw the potential damage that could be done,
the man immediately set out to protect his house,
shuttering the windows and bolting the doors.
He told himself after the rains, he would take them down,
but when the rains stopped, the walls remained.
There was safety in their protection,
and a security in no longer feeling at the mercy
of the storms that had alarmed him.

"He no longer ventured out,
reasoning the storms could return at any time,
and though they stayed away,
he continued to stay home, preferring to be shuttered in.
Days turned into weeks,
weeks into months, and months into years.
When his supplies ran out,
he had no option but to leave the comfort of his home
to get more food.

"The thought terrified him.
He had grown so used to being shut in
that the thought of venturing outside made him anxious.

"Looking back, he recalled when he had first come to this place:
how he had loved the light
and the feeling of openness and freedom.
He wondered how he had let himself get to this place.
It was in that moment that he understood
the power that fear had over him.

"In protecting himself from the storms, he had shut down.
Barricaded in, separated from everything he once enjoyed,
his palace had become his prison.
'Enough!' he cried.
One by one, he opened the shutters
and unbolted the doors.
Light streamed into his house again;
just as it had always done in the past.
And once again, his heart was filled with happiness."

Entranced by the tale,
it took Mo several moments to return to present awareness.

"Mo, the man in this story is you," The Bodyguard gently counseled.
"Just like him, you were on a search to find something
and when you found it, you, like the man in the story, enjoyed it.
And then a storm came,
and took away the love you had craved for so long.
The loss of those you loved,
and the suffering your sensitive soul was forced to endure

resurfaced again
when you lost The Flower Girl.

"You have certainly been given your share of storms.
And it is no wonder you got scared, Mo.
And then when that fear was rekindled,
and The Beast came,
you tried again to lock a part of yourself behind those walls.

"But those walls can protect you no longer.
The Beast has been released,
and just as you used those walls to take away his freedom,
he is now using them to keep what you want from coming to you.

"That wall separates one piece of you from another piece of you.
It is time to connect those pieces together again."

"How do I do that?" Mo asked.
And he heard a voice inside him answer,
'Put on the shoes.'

The Bodyguard continued as the sun rose high in the sky:
"For many years, I was the biggest and the strongest.
People hired me to do exactly
what you tried to have your walls do for you.
And for many years, I kept them safe.

"Until the day I met The Wise One.
He was different.
He was not afraid of me, like all the others had been.
He saw through me.

"He saw the walls I had around me
were to protect me from my own attacks.
He found that scared place inside me,
and taught me to be kind to myself."

Mo could barely speak,
completely absorbed in the presence of love.
He basked in it,
and not only allowed it to enter him,
but to pour forth from him.

Suddenly, Mo felt no separation. No walls.

The Bodyguard smiled and asked Mo to give him his shoes.
Reaching for his foot as if he were reaching into Mo's soul,
The Bodyguard put one shoe on Mo's foot
and then the other.

When he took his hand away,
The Beast was standing before them.

Mo stood there for some time in this ineffable state of love,
and when The Bodyguard finally walked away,
The Beast re-entered Mo and they walked together once again.
Only this time, each was an important part of the other.

Gone with The Bodyguard
was the feeling of separation he had felt his whole life.
For the first time,
Mo felt completely connected to his Beast and the world around him.

And in this connection, Mo could *feel*.
He *knew* if people were happy or sad,
but even more, he could feel what their bodies felt.

As the passerby approached,
Mo's heart tightened.
He could feel the man's constricted veins
having trouble pumping blood around his body.
Mo felt this constriction in his body.
As the man passed, the sensation passed with him,
and Mo's heart felt better.

Moments later without warning, Mo's knee buckled beneath him
and he fell to the ground,
the pain excruciating.
And then, equally curiously, it was gone,
just as Mo noticed the limping man walk past him.

Still lying on the ground,
Mo saw the face of someone who made him very happy.
There, sitting down next to him was The Wise One.

THE WISE ONE

He sat on the ground next to Mo
and thought about how their relationship had changed.
When they had first met, Mo had been so arrogant.

The Wise One understood that it had been his way of protecting himself.
The walls that Mo had put up were not of superiority but of weakness.
Mo had learned a lot on his journey.
He no longer felt the need to hide his weakness
or lock up his strength.

As The Wise One looked at him now,
he saw that Mo was becoming the man he had known he would become.
It warmed his soul
to know that what had been set in motion so many years ago
was now coming to fruition.

He liked Mo's unpredictability.
And that he was willing to risk everything in his search for heaven.
The Wise One saw a part of him had already died,
and something new was filling him.
This was very good.
Now, he wanted to sit with Mo and see how he was doing.

It took only seconds for The Wise One to see what he was looking to find.
He knew Mo was strong,
but the journey that remained was extremely challenging.
He wondered: "Would Mo be able to get through to the other side?"

As The Wise One looked Mo in the eye,
he simply asked: "How are you, Mo?"

Mo answered honestly:

"I am tired.

This trip has taken a lot longer and been a lot harder than I thought.

Emotionally, it is far more challenging than I would have ever imagined.

"I am still nowhere near to finding heaven,

and I have lost more than I have gained.

Seeing you now, I realize how lost I am.

I do not know if I can make it.

Maybe it's time to give up this search.

Maybe I'm not supposed to have the things I think I should have.

Everything I have ever loved has been taken from me,

and even when I had The Flower Girl, she left me."

The Wise One listened.

He wondered if now was the time to share with Mo his destiny,

but the more he heard him speak,

the more he realized

Mo needed more time.

There were still a lot of things he needed to work out.

For what was being asked of him, he needed to be all in,

and now as he spoke,

The Wise One felt Mo's indecision.

It was natural for people to feel some hesitation.

It was something everyone experienced,

but at this moment, after all Mo had been through,

he was not sure how many more disappointments Mo could take

before he would give up on finding The Mosaic.

The Wise One knew the most important thing for Mo
was to find The Flower Girl,
but in order for that to happen,
he needed to do something.

THE THIEF

When Mo looked up again,
The Wise One was gone.
He was now on a crowded street
in the center of a big city.
He couldn't believe what he was seeing.

Out of the corner of his eye,
on the other side of the busy street,
a man was stealing a wallet
from the pocket of a passerby.
Just as Mo was about to leap forward
to intercept the crime,
The Thief quickly slid the wallet back into the man's pocket,
all without the man's knowledge.

Shocked, Mo stood motionless,
watching The Thief steal from people again and again,
only to return what he stole so quickly
his victims were none the wiser.

*"Why would someone steal something
and then immediately give it back —
not just once, but many times?"* mused Mo.
It didn't make sense.

Mo turned his head for a moment,
and when he looked back, The Thief was gone.
It was only then that
he felt the lightning fast hand of The Thief
reaching into his pocket,
taking his wallet.

"Hey!" Mo shouted.
But before the sound left his mouth,
The Thief was already running away.
Mo took off after him.
They ran for quite a while,
and it surprised Mo
that as fast as The Thief ran,
he was able to keep him in sight.

When they reached a more secluded area,
The Thief stopped running and turned to face Mo.
"Here is your wallet. I am sorry I took it,"
The Thief said, extending his hand with the wallet

"But I saw you watching me
and needed to get you away from the crowd
before you ruined everything.
I have work I have come to do;
I do not have a lot of time.
Listen carefully."

"No," Mo said,
as he stood there winded, trying to catch his breath.
"You listen. I need an answer.
Why do you steal something
only to give it back?"

The Thief replied,
"I do not give back just what I take.
Look in your wallet, Mo."

Mo opened his wallet
and found it filled with money,
a lot more than had been in it before it had been stolen.

"How did all this money get in my wallet?" Mo asked.
"I don't understand.
Who are you and what are you doing?"

"I am a Thief.
I was taught by the best
how to steal from people without them ever knowing.

"I stole their possessions
through business deals I made,
in which I prospered and they lost.
I stole their houses
when they lost money
and could no longer pay their mortgages.
I stole their time,
by making them wait,
asking them to give me more and more information
and then never giving them anything back.

"Somehow, without realizing it,
I was the one who lost everything.
I became financially rich and well known,
but poor in every other aspect of my life.
I lost everything.
As I secretly took from others,
I didn't realize my values were being taken from me.

"It was then, in my darkest moment,
when there was nothing left to lose,
that he came and stole from me."

"What can you steal from a man who has nothing?" Mo asked.

The Thief turned to leave and then answered,
"He stole my suffering.
On that day
I decided to steal what cannot be seen.
I steal the thoughts people have
that keep them from doing what they came to do.
I steal the connections people make that cause them pain,
and the fear they have that causes them to hesitate."

Mo looked at The Thief and asked,
"When you took my wallet,
what did you steal from me?"

The Thief replied,
"A good thief never tells someone what he steals.
He only hopes that it is valuable enough
that when it is gone,
the one he has stolen it from notices it is no longer there.
The first of those things, I have already accomplished;
now I must see if what I took
is valuable enough that you feel its absence."

Mo didn't like The Thief,
but The Beast hated him
and the rage inside him started to boil.

"No one steals from me,"
said The Beast.

As Mo tried to calm The Beast,
he realized he did not even know what The Thief had taken.
All The Beast knew was that he felt something missing.
Mo did, too, but neither of them knew what it was.

Mo checked his belongings,
which took almost no time at all
because of how little Mo actually had.
He thought about that for the briefest of moments,
wondering how he had functioned so well with so little,
but he did not allow his mind to wander there for long
because he needed to know,
of the little he did have, what had been stolen.

He was happy his shoes were still on his feet,
and the little he did have in his wallet
he already saw had been multiplied 100 times.
It seemed he had ended up better than he started,
and he thought to go and celebrate,
to listen to some music and have good food and drink,
but it bothered him
to know that The Thief had taken something from him
and to not know what it was.

Again and again he did a mental inventory of everything he owned.
It was all still there.
When there was nothing else left to check,
Mo remembered that The Thief said
he now stole things no one could see.

So he checked his mind to see if he still had his thoughts and beliefs.
He remembered years ago being shown a technique
that helped him change the thoughts he focused on.

He wondered if he might use that technique now
to do a mental inventory.
Many years ago, just after his father died,
a woman had shown him
how to minimize the things that were stealing his peace,
and to maximize that which brought him happiness.

She said, "See your thoughts and beliefs as images in the mind.
For the things you no longer want to believe,
click on them, as if they were images on your computer.
shrink them down and move them to the back corner of the screen.

"Then one by one, find the images that bring you joy.
Click on those and expand them.
Make them into color images
and bring those big images front and center."

Mo wondered if he could use this technique
just to bring all the things he thought and believed forward.
The first thought that came was of The Flower Girl.
Thankfully, The Thief had not stolen her.
Nor did he steal the thought of marrying her
and starting a family or of finding heaven.
All of these thoughts remained,
and Mo wondered what was so valuable
that The Thief would steal it from Mo.
As the nights become shorter and the days stretched longer,

Mo walked west in search of heaven and The Flower Girl.
Still, he tried to find what no longer existed,
all the while not even seeing what was right in front of him.

Mo played the scenario over and over in his mind.
"I watched him steal.
Every time he took something from someone,
he immediately replaced what he took
and no one even knew he took anything.

"I not only watched him do that to others,
I watched him do it to me.
My wallet came back to me with 100x more money in it
than when he initially took it.
Hold on, hold on,
as he pulled his wallet out to look through it again.
"Maybe I missed something."
He had looked through the wallet many times,
but there in the back, behind other things, was a card.

Slowly, with hands trembling a bit he pulled out the card
and gently unfolded it.
There before his eyes, he saw it.
Folded up inside the card was a piece of paper
with this message written on it:

■ ■ ■ ■ ■

THE LOVER

"Open your heart.
The Lover knows your pain, your longing, and your suffering,
and still she invites you to experience living from a place of love.
You want her, but she wants you one million times more.
What you seek right now is circling around you,
looking for a way to enter, but you cannot see her.
You sit before the door to a new universe,
but have no idea how to unlock it.
Your door is locked. Your windows are closed.
It is time to open up everything.

"The Lover asks you to love with risk,
to go beyond where you are comfortable.
If you stay where you are, you will never find her.

"The Mosaic is calling you to find the connection
from the known to the unknown,
where magic happens and miracles abound.

"Time. Space. Energy. Matter.
When The Lover calls you, you must heed her call.
Find a way, if necessary, to cross parallel realities to find her.
There can be no happiness without her,
and there is nowhere else you belong than in her arms.
Celebrate. A portal will soon open.
When it does, you must walk through."

Mo felt the truth of these words.
He was being pulled toward something new,
and he told himself over and over again,
"just keep walking."

THE GARDENER

As evening came,
Mo found a place to rest
on the outskirts of the village.
As he watched the sun set and the evening begin,
his senses were teased by a heady aroma
that drifted on the night air toward him.

It was only on the following morning
as he entered the town,
that he was struck by the glorious
sight of the aroma's source.

The village was an explosion of flowers,
a barrage of color,
an array of elegance
such that he had never before seen.
Each flower was exquisitely placed
within immaculately trimmed gardens.

Stunned, he could only stand and stare
as his eyes feasted on the sight of pure perfection.

The meticulousness of the manicured gardens,
the sharpness and the brilliance of the colors
that played upon each other
made each flower more beautiful than the last.
Mo's senses were so intoxicated
he had to sit for a while to allow the cells of his body
to absorb the sight and the scent of them.

Instinctively, he closed his eyes,
wanting to feel this place even more deeply.

When he finally opened them
his gaze was arrested by another sight —
a man standing barely a few inches away
looking quizzically at him.

Startled, Mo asked,
"Who are you?"

"I am The Gardener," the man replied, smiling.

"Is it your vision that created these gardens?
If so, I would like to see the world through your eyes.
They are impeccable
and this beauty you've created is other-worldly.
How do you make things so beautiful?" Mo asked.

"Creating a beautiful garden is easy," The Gardener said,
"because there is so little I need do.
Each flower on its own is magnificent.
My job is not to create beauty,
but to see the beauty that already is.
I simply clear a space
for the beauty of nature to be appreciated more fully.
So you see, I do nothing."

"But…but…" Mo stumbled on.
"These gardens are stunning.
Surely there is more to it than that."

"If I do anything," said The Gardener,
"it is simply to find the right combination
that enables each to make the other more beautiful.

And though this takes some skill,
anyone with an eye and a feel for beauty can do the same."

Mo was still perplexed.
Surely The Gardener did more than nothing.
He had traveled to many beautiful gardens
and nothing he had ever seen
came close to the beauty that enveloped him now.

"But, surely," he stammered,
you must do more than that;
arrangement alone could not possibly create such beauty."

"Ahhhhh," The Gardener smiled.
"Have you ever planted a garden?"

"Yes I have," Mo answered,
thinking of the small plot behind his childhood home.

Asked The Gardener, "When you weeded your garden
and you pulled at the weeds,
what did you do with the ones that broke off at ground level?"

Mo answered honestly.

"Usually, I just cut them so they could not be seen
and continued weeding the rest of the garden.
I knew that I should have pulled them out,
but I did not have the patience
to get all those weeds out from their roots."

"I understand," The Gardener said.
"I am a Gardener.
I have nothing else I have to do,
so I do what others do not:
I remove those weeds.

"A garden is made beautiful
not only because of what you see
but also because of what you do *not* see.
When you weed a garden,
but do not pull the weed out at the root,
the weed remains and the root gets stronger.
So when you water your garden,
you nourish both the flower and the weed.
I am in no rush.
I have nowhere else to be but in my garden.
So when I find a weed
that does not come out with a gentle pull,
I dig, and dig,
and I do not stop until I get to the root
and remove it.

"Weeds will always grow in the garden,
but a true gardener watches his garden.
When he finds something that does not belong,
he immediately pulls it out
before its roots have a chance to grow.
When I take away what does not belong,
what does belong grows,
and an aroma arises from my garden that captivates the senses.

"Perhaps what you see is what you don't see."

Finally, Mo smiled with understanding.
He remembered a wise man once telling him,

"Look at the window.
When it is dirty, you cannot see through it.
But when it is clean, you see what lies beyond.
The beauty of the window is that you do not see it."

Something about The Gardener reminded Mo of that wise man.
His message of the beauty of being invisible touched Mo
and he said to him,

"Please stay with me a while.
I have watched as people come and go,
and often they leave before I have a chance to find out more.
May I ask you a few questions?"

The Gardener grinned, sat next to Mo and said,

"I do not know if I will be able to answer your questions
but ask me whatever you like and I will do my best to bring insight."

Mo told him the story of The Flower Girl.
He told him how he had thought he would never lose her
and how suddenly she had slipped away.
And as Mo spoke,
The Gardener heard his fear.
He asked Mo about it.

Mo told him as much as he loved The Flower Girl,
he knew nothing of the world she lived in.
He told The Gardener he felt like he was standing

on the edge of everything he had ever wanted
but was too scared to jump in.

The Gardener completely understood,
and yet in an innocent voice
He said only, "Why?"

Mo told him of his journey
and how many times he had thought to turn back.
He told him that everything he had ever loved had been taken from him
and that he was scared to give himself to someone again.
He told him that if he were to lose The Flower Girl again,
it would be more than he could handle,
but he knew only with her would he be able to fulfill his purpose.
And then he asked The Gardener
if he knew how to access the other dimension,
for he was sure she was there waiting for him.

The Gardener smiled.
He could feel the love he felt for The Flower Girl.
He knew a love this strong
had the power to propel one across the dimensions of time and space,
and He saw the weed in his garden that was keeping him from crossing.
It was fear.

But here was the crazy thing:
When he went to pull the weed, it was not there.
He had never seen anything like this before.
Mo was sure the fear was there
and when he told him it wasn't there anymore,
he was bewildered.

He asked,
"Then what is keeping me from seeing the other dimension?"

The Gardener answered,
"Your belief that the fear is there, even though it is gone,
keeps you thinking it is still there.
But how could it have been taken without your knowing?" he asked.

Mo closed his eyes for a moment to ponder his question.
He smiled.
What he saw with his eyes closed
was The Thief standing in front of him,
laughing, holding the weed in his hand.

"It's about time you figured it out, Mo.
I told you I am a very good thief," The Thief said to him.

Mo opened his eyes and wanted to explain
all that had happened to The Gardener,
but he was gone.

THE MONK

Mo closed his eyes again and remembered the words of The Traveler:
"When you fall out of sync . . . you become disconnected.
And when you feel disconnected, you suffer."

Mo had been disconnected from himself
and now that he knew the weed of his fear was gone,
his garden was clean and he was happy.
His journey had brought him
to where the wild, cold ocean waves crashed against the land.
As he sat listening to the seabirds with closed eyes,
The Monk with the face like sunshine
and the begging bowl in his hand
walked right up to him and tapped him on his shoulder.
Without a second thought,
Mo reached into his pocket
and gave him a large bill.

The Monk smiled
and thanked Mo for his generosity.
But it was Mo who continued,
"I can see from your eyes
and the smile on your face
that you have found what I seek.
How do I find it?"

"It is not something you must look for
nor is it something you need to find.
It is here, right in front of you.
The fact that you cannot see it means
you have not been shown how to enter the other dimension."
The seriousness of the Monk's words
was offset by the joy pouring forth from his eyes.

"Where?" asked Mo, looking around him.
"I do not see it."

The Monk could no longer contain
the merriment that bubbled within him.
His laugh started at the base of his belly
and came all the way up.

He was not laughing at Mo,
but at the absurdity of the question.

With a gentle touch on Mo's arm,
and a loving smile, he whispered,
"You cannot find that which is inside, outside.
You must go within."

Craving an answer, Mo asked,
"How do I do that?
How do I find what is within?
Can you teach me?"

The Monk smiled.
"I can show you the door," he said,
"but you must walk through it on your own.
You are the way. Remember that.
No matter how often you get distracted,
return to where you are."

"I am ready," Mo affirmed eagerly.
"Please take me to the door."

And there in the busy beach town,
everything vanished.

All that remained was the two of them
standing in front of a slice in time,
a door between one world and another.

Mo listened intently
as the Monk spoke to him
of the four breaths.

He closed his eyes
and took a deep inhalation
followed by a deep exhalation.
He did it again and again.

On the fifth exhalation,
the Monk unzipped the sky
and Mo crossed through the space that had opened.
Suddenly, he was on the other side.

THE WAITRESS

He was puzzled.
Mo knew nothing about how a parallel reality worked,
but he wondered why of all possible places to greet him
in this new reality
would there be a restaurant.

He had fantasized that the moment he crossed the portal,
The Flower Girl would be there waiting for him
and that she would come running into his outstretched arms
just as he had done
as a boy waiting for his dad to come home from work.
But that was not what happened.

He was sitting alone in a diner.
The good news? The place was bustling and busy
and everyone seemed happy with the food they were getting.

Minutes after he was seated,
The Waitress came and took his order.
She returned moments later with a scrumptious country breakfast
that made Mo's mouth water.

"Wow. That was fast.
I hadn't realized until this moment how hungry I was.
Thank you for bringing my food so quickly,"
he said, as he ate with the blind hunger
of one who had not eaten for days.

*"Is it possible
that my hunger could have created this place?
Maybe that is how a parallel reality works,"* he thought.

The Flower Girl was heartbroken
that Mo had not recognized her.
She had hoped that he would see her eyes and know it was she.
But he had not.
She went back again to continue the conversation,
asking if everything was ok.
Still not recognizing her,
Mo spoke about the food
rather than himself, which is what she had intended, saying,
"Yes, it is wonderful. Everything tastes great.
There is something about this food
that not only nourishes my body but somehow soothes my soul."

The Waitress smiled.
"People come here hungry.
We give them not only what they want,
we give them what they need.

"It seems everyone is looking for something.
Some find what they are looking for here
right in front of them,
while others come and go without ever seeing anything."

Her words somehow reminded him of the words of his father:
"Do not get distracted by how they look or what they do.
Nothing is as it seems."

And then, he saw her.
He could not believe how tricky the mind is.
She was no longer The Waitress serving food in a restaurant,
she was The Flower Girl standing in front of her flower shop
reaching out to offer him a rose.

THE FLOWER GIRL

Time, space, form.
Everything melted as Mo ran to her.
Tears flowed from his eyes,
not tears of sorrow but of immeasurable joy.

Inside him, The Beast roared. And The Flower Girl shuddered.
He had done it,
he had passed through all of the obstacles
and found her.

She had known when she released him
that she had taken a chance,
but she believed in their love so much
that she knew he would come.
He and The Beast had crossed dimensions to find her.
And now she would never lose him again.

The Clairvoyant had been wrong.

The Flower Girl was right for him.
And even so,
everything had needed to fall perfectly in place
in order for it to happen.
Mo had suffered a lot
and through the experience of so many trials
and so much pain,
he had come to find peace with The Beast
and to trust him.

The Flower Girl knew she had devastated him when she left him,
but she loved him so much
that she was willing to sacrifice her own happiness

to give Mo the opportunity to get past this last hurdle.
She was willing to be seen forever
as the one who broke his heart
if he did not pass this test.
But he did. She was so proud of him.

He had trusted in the power of their love
and it melted every obstacle.

He had done what only a few have ever been able to do,
change the destiny of The Clairvoyant.

The Wise One smiled.

THE WISE ONE

And then suddenly, Mo was in a sun-dappled room full of people.
Open French doors led out onto a sloping green lawn
that seemed to go on forever.
The Flower Girl was "talking" at one end of the room.
Only a few words left her lips
as people gathered around her.
They had not come to hear her words.

They came to experience her love.
And as she embraced each one,
she offered them a flower and said,
"Love melts everything."

As The Flower Girl finished,
The Gifted Child stood as if on cue,
her movements awkward,
her language garbled.
Her "words" came not from her mouth, but from her heart,
and entered into the hearts of those who heard her silence.

"Love each other.
On the surface, you are as different to me as I am to you,
but underneath, we are the same.
It is all an illusion.
We are not separate.
We are all connected."

As the Gifted Child finished,
awe filled the room.

The Wise One rose from a deep armchair.
As he walked, he stopped to share with some a personal message.

Between his words to individuals, he spoke the mantra
sometimes only once, sometimes over and over again:

"When we are connected, we are happy.
When we are disconnected, we suffer.
This is The Mosaic."

When he finished, he moved to the next person.
With some, he spent only moments;
with others, he stayed longer.

But somehow each got exactly what he or she needed.
Each time he would leave, before going on to the next,
he would say again,

"When we are connected, we are happy.
When we are disconnected, we suffer.
This is The Mosaic."

Mo thought back on the journey that had brought him here.
So many years had passed.
He had left home as a boy,
completely disconnected from the world around him.
Now he was a man, older and wiser in so many ways.

He thought about the words of The Street Artist,
"It is our brokenness that makes us beautiful."
Mo had wanted so much to believe him,
but all his life, Mo had felt lost in his brokenness --
so much so that when he left on his journey years ago,
the only memory he took with him
was a broken picture frame that had once held a picture of his dad.

He had carried the pieces with him on his walk
to remind him of the connection he had with his dad.
When he lost his bearings,
he would pull out the pieces and look at them,
and each time he did, they told him
to find that which would allow him to feel connected again.

As he sat here now, in the arms of The Flower Girl,
he felt closer than he'd ever been,
and still he longed to re-experience
that connection to all of creation The Wise One had shared with him.

He had told Mo
all those years ago
that one day he would re-connect him to the living Mosaic,
and Mo could not help but hope as The Wise One came closer
that this was the moment it would happen.

He put his hand in his pocket to grasp the broken pieces,
but nothing could have prepared him
for what was about to happen next --
the pieces were gone.

As The Wise One approached,
The Flower Girl turned to walk away,
but Mo held her close and asked The Wise One,
"Can she stay?"

The Wise One responded,
"You have changed destiny. You are now its maker.
If you want The Flower Girl to stay, she can stay."

The Wise One then continued,
"I have been watching you.
From the moment we met
years ago in the hills,
I have been following you.

"You asked me then for a blessing I could not give you.
But I have walked with you,
through your triumphs and your adversities.
I listened as people told you their stories,
and I saw the way you interacted
and the respect you showed to all.

"All that time, I watched you . . .
I had to be sure you were the one.
And there were times I questioned you.
Times when you sought The Flower Girl, for instance,
and I myself thought you had gone astray.
But as I continued to watch you, I learned from you.

"You have always impressed me, Mo.
I have waited a long time for this moment,
for you to be ready,
and now that time has come."

With those words,
The Wise One reached out and embraced Mo.
The Flower Girl instinctively stepped back
and stood to the side as to not interrupt,
but Mo again invited her into the embrace.

Connected now to The Wise One and The Flower Girl,
Mo felt that impenetrable force once again enter him.
But it was different now.
The first time, information had been drawn from him;
this time, the wisdom of The Wise One was pouring into him.

With each passing second, Mo felt the presence increasing.
He looked to The Flower Girl,
her eyes filled with a joy he had not seen before.

As he looked over to The Wise One,
his smile spoke of a love that could not be captured in time.
Past, present, and future all danced together in parallel realities.
And all of it was a confirmation to The Wise One that Mo was ready.

It was time for the world to know The Mosaic.
And Mo was the one to be its messenger.

Even now, as the energy entered him,
Mo tried to downplay his part in it,
telling The Wise One,
"I am an ordinary man.
The work you speak of is done by those who are special."

The Wise One looked at Mo and said to him,
"Your humility is beautiful,
but never allow it to become a hiding place
for you to shrink from your greatness.
It is time to do what you were created to do.

"On your walk, you met many people --
Ordinaries who were anything but ordinary.

"The artistry of The Mosaic draws no distinction among people.
It connects all pieces: big, small, broken, whole, shiny or dull.
It is the blending of colors, textures and materials.
that makes The Mosaic so beautiful."

"But what holds the pieces of The Mosaic together?" Mo asked.

The Wise One laughed and laughed
until his laugh eased into a smile and he answered Mo, saying,
"The Mosaic is whole, not broken,
so there is nothing it needs to hold it together."

"But what of all these broken pieces we see?" Mo continued.
"The pieces that make up The Mosaic."

"Ah," The Wise One answered,
"this is the big lie, the great illusion.
We think what we see is real,
so we believe the world is separate.
But, remember, what we see is only what we see;
In reality, everything is connected.

Separateness is the great illusion of this reality.
Mo, you experienced the oneness of The Mosaic.
You know we are all connected,
and even now, you think things are separate.
That is the power of the illusion.
I have walked with you on your walk, and I have watched you.
Without knowing it, you practiced the initiation of connection.
You sat with the people you met,
and you listened to them.
This is what connects people.

"There is a beauty in the ones who go unnoticed.
Spend time with them and listen to their stories.
The more you listen,
the more they will tell you.
And if you ask them
why so many feel broken and disconnected,
they just might share with you what is needed to connect the world again.

"There will be those who will tell you
it is impossible to reconnect a disconnected world.
They will tell you it is too late, that what is broken is irreparable.
The only reason they believe it is impossible
is because they have not yet seen a way to make it possible.
By gathering together
those of like and unlike minds,
each will show the other the world they see,
and if we listen to each other,
we will see what we have never seen before,
and perhaps the impossible will suddenly become possible.
It is in this place that innovation, magic, and miracles exist.
This is The Mosaic."

This was The Wise One's final initiation.
With that, the days of The Wise One ended . . .
and the days of Mo began.

The Wise One sat down,
and now as Mo walked around the room,
he repeated the message of The Wise One to all:
"Connected, we are happy.
Disconnected, we suffer.
This is The Mosaic."

Mo now understood
what had once isolated him and made him feel so alone,
the very thing that made him so different—
his ability to see what others couldn't see—
was now the very thing
needed to connect the disconnected.

Walking around the room,
he was overwhelmed by a feeling of immense gratitude.
As he approached the man with the familiar face
who sat awaiting his blessing,
Mo gave him the biggest, fullest hug a man could ever give.
The smile on his face was radiant.
There sitting before him
was his dad.

After all these years, all the doubts,
all the thoughts of giving up,
he had found him.
Tears filled their eyes.
His dad looked at him and said,
"I am so proud of you, Mo.
Against great odds, you found me.
But know this, Mo, everywhere you went,
I was with you.
Though you couldn't see me,
I was always with you."

As his dad finished speaking,
Mo saw the face of his dad change.
In it, he saw the faces of

The Road Worker
The Juiceman
The Traveler
The Wise One, oh The Wise One.
Mo watched, as one by one, the faces of all those he met on his walk
now metamorphosed into the face of his dad.
But when the faces had all come and gone
There remained one person Mo had not seen.
his mother.

He asked his dad if she was here, if she had found him.
And just when Mo was about to tell him how she suffered,
another veil lifted
and he saw his mother sitting right beside his dad.

Mo hugged them until he had no strength left.
And then they just started laughing.
The troubles that had once ruled their world were gone.
Somewhere in the vast continuum of time,
for a moment at least, all suffering ended.

Time stopped, distance vanished.
Past, present, future all connected in this moment.
It was as it had always been:
and they laughed together until late into the night.
But this time there was one difference,
The woman he loved was sitting right beside him.
As Mo looked again at his dad,
he noticed a picture on the side table behind him.
There, looking right at him, was the picture of his dad
in the broken frame he had carried with him his whole trip.
But somehow the frame was now whole.

It was then that he heard the whisper of The Wise One,
"Nothing is broken, Mo.
It is all just an illusion.
Everything is connected."

ABOUT THE AUTHOR

DANIEL LEVIN lost his parents as a boy two years apart on the same day, and only realized while writing THE MOSAIC that he has spent his whole life searching for the place the adults called heaven.

He thought he had found this heaven when his uncle, who started a company that was a household name saw in him the potential to one day run it and offered him the chance to start at the bottom and work his way up to the top. But as generous as his uncle's offer was, Levin soon realized it was not the heaven he was looking to find.

Levin was the prodigy of the man who founded Organizational Psychology and he wanted Levin to help him develop and grow it, but once again, he saw the answers he sought were not there.

He has hitchhiked around the world, started businesses, grown businesses and lost a business too. He donated all of his money to the poor, thinking their need was greater than his. His life has been a mix of amazing highs and tumultuous lows.

He has travelled to many different countries and dined with the richest of the rich and sat on street corners with the poorest of the poor. All the while, he has observed that no matter what country people come from, or where they are economically, no matter what color their skin or what religion they practice, we are all the same. We all want to be loved and accepted, listened to and understood, acknowledge and validated.

Levin finally found his heaven in his connection to THE MOSAIC. He speaks of this in his workshops, retreats, online courses, and Mosaic coaching. He hopes you will join him on his mission to reconnect a disconnected world.

ABOUT THE ARTISTS:

Credit: Source -Juan Olmo
Pinterest Mosaicos Coqui
Archetype: The Programmer

Artist: Stephen Brailo – http://www.brailomosaics.com
Mosaic: Girl with a Vase
Archetype: The Flower Girl

Artist: Gary Drostle - Website: www.drostle.com
Mosaic: Robeson - Location: Gallery Works, Private Collection UK
Archetype: The Road Worker
Mosaic: Outside the Lines Location: Gallery Works,International Mosaic
Archetype: The Thief

Artist: Armando Heredia,
https://www.flickr.com/photos/cardboardastronaut/3287197143
Mosaic: Detail of a Mosaic of Moses
Archetype: The Wise One

Artist: Carlos Cohen,
Website: www.MosaicMasters.com
Mosaic: Samurai
Archetype: The Mirror Maker
Mosaic: El Arabe II
Archetype: The Juiceman
Mosaic: Geisha
Archetype: The Traveler

Artist: Jason Cohen - Website: www.MosaicMasters.com
Mosaic: La Arabe
Archetype: The Mortician

ABOUT THE BOOK

THE MOSAIC is a simple story
and just like the characters the story introduces,
when we sit with it,
we soon realize there might be more to it than we initially saw.
In a book that speaks about seeing what we do not see,
it should not take the reader completely by surprise
even in this simple fable, that what we initially see may not be all that is.

The fact that you are holding this book in your hands
means THE MOSAIC has come for you,
and invites you to ask yourself this simple question,
"What would we see if we could see what we do not see?"
How would that impact every part of our lives,
our relationships, businesses, families, and the way we educate our children?
Our politics; and the way we treat each other?
How would the ability to see differently
impact the global wellbeing of the world?

THE MOSAIC is a book about connection
to ourselves, our source, our purpose, our planet and to each other.
It is about seeing the connection to everything,
time and space; past, present and future
and about how those connections shape the world we live in.
The mission of THE MOSAIC is to reconnect a disconnected world
for its simple premise is in connection, there is happiness;
in disconnection, there is suffering.

May this simple little story be a catalyst to bring us together
so that we see we are not separate. We are all connected.

BE KIND
TO YOURSELF

BE VULNERABLE

DO WHAT YOU
CAME TO DO

BUILD YOUR MOSAIC